Mr Penguin's adventures began in:

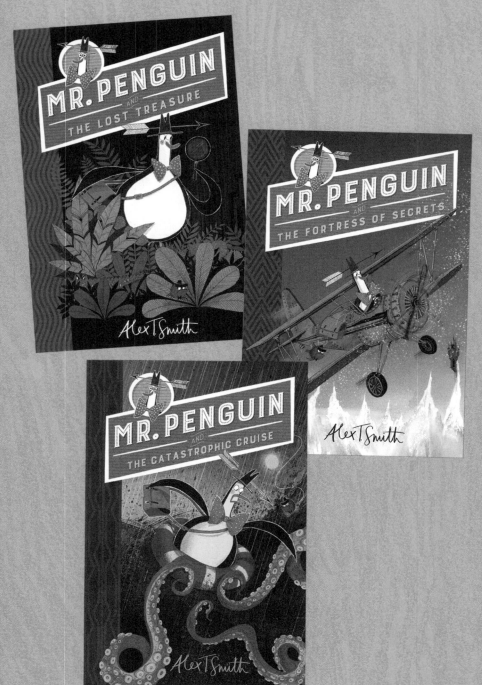

ALEX T. SMITH

h HODDER

Mr Penguin is a penguin.

If you aren't sure whether he is one or not,
all you have to do is look at him.
Here he is now.

He *looks* like a penguin.

He is all black and white with a little beak
and two flappy flippers. When he walks, his
bottom wiggles about in *exactly* the sort of
way a penguin's bottom *should* wiggle.
But there's something rather unusual about
Mr Penguin. You see, he isn't
JUST a penguin.

He is an *Adventurer!*

He has the dashing hat, enormous magnifying glass and battered satchel – with a nice packed lunch of fish finger sandwiches inside – to prove it.

Mr Penguin's best friend is this spider. His name is Colin. He's really good at kung fu, so you'd better watch out! KAPOW!

That woman with the headscarf – she's called Edith Hedge. She's Mr Penguin's other best friend. The pigeon on her head is Gordon. He doesn't say much.

Together, they've been on three thrilling adventures already. Are you ready to join them on another?

For Mr Connor, Detective and Penguin.
With love from Mr Uncle Alex

HODDER CHILDREN'S BOOKS
First published in Great Britain in 2021 by Hodder & Stoughton

1 3 5 7 9 10 8 6 4 2

Text and illustrations copyright © Alex T. Smith, 2021

The moral rights of the author have been asserted.

A CIP catalogue record for this book is available from the British Library.

978 1 444 94460 0

Design by Alison Still

Printed and bound in Italy by Printer Trento S.r.l.

The paper and board used in this book are made from wood from
responsible sources.

Hodder Children's Books
A division of Hachette Children's Group
Carmelite House, 50 Victoria Embankment, London EC4Y 0DZ

An Hachette UK Company
www.hachette.co.uk

CONTENTS

*I*t was a strange night in the city, made even stranger by a filthy fog that slithered down the alleyways like an eerie, ghostly snake. Trees shivered in its wake.

The mist rolled down a side street and up the steps of a tall, thin building. A sign outside announced it as the Museum of Ancient Thingamajigs. The place was in darkness except for a single light in a window on the top floor, the office of the director of the museum, Dr Bernard Fossil. He was sitting at his desk in a very bad mood.

For the five hundred and ninth time that evening he took out his pocket watch, looked at the time then harrumphed through his bristly nose.

11.45 p.m.! His special delivery was meant to have been delivered HOURS ago!

"Well, it won't come now," he grunted, and he was getting himself ready to go home in a most irritable manner… when there suddenly came a loud knocking on the museum's front door.

"What time do they call this?" snorted Dr Fossil, plonking his hat on to his shiny head. Even though he was annoyed, he felt a quiver of excitement. It was finally here!

He hoofed it down the large curving staircase at speed and unbolted the locks with large, fumbling fingers. Yes, there it was on the doorstep! He could hardly contain himself!

A portly man in a delivery driver's uniform and with a cap pulled low over his face thrust a piece of paper into his hand and grunted "SIGN PLEASE." Dr Fossil had hardly handed it back when the driver hopped into his van and zoomed off into the foggy night.

"Aren't you going to help me bring it inside?" cried Dr Fossil to the vanishing exhaust fumes. "Obviously not…" he harrumphed, and set to work heaving and pushing the large, heavy package into the museum. Finally, he gave it a shove across the polished floor of the entrance hall and it came to a stop, lit up by a shaft of moonlight coming through one of the high windows.

Fossil set about opening the wooden crate, with the help of a crowbar. After a few minutes' work, and a final splintering crunch, the lid was off and the item inside was revealed.

It was wonderful!

Dr Fossil's little eyes gleamed as he looked at the ancient sarcophagus. The large stone coffin was covered in masses of gold and glittered with hundreds, no, THOUSANDS of gems.

And now, thought Dr Fossil, grinning, it belongs to ME!

His pocket watch chimed midnight, making Dr Fossil blink himself out of his excitement. He really must go home, but he decided that he would set his alarm clock extra early so he could look at his new prize before the museum opened. With one last glance, he wiggled out of the front door, slammed it shut and locked the whole place up tight.

For several minutes the museum sat in dark silence. Some of the fog from outside had slipped through the door and now wafted around the new delivery like it had been drawn to it.

Had there been anyone in the room to watch, they would have seen something extraordinary happen. Slowly, very slowly, the lid of the sarcophagus started to lift. Then, *in a cloud of billowing dust, a dark figure unravelled themselves. They clambered out of the coffin and tiptoed sneakily off into the museum – past the Hall of Unidentified Whatsits and past the Room of We Don't Know What These Things Are, before stopping outside a heavy door. The sign above read* The Private Collection of Dr Bernard Fossil KEEP OUT.

The figure pulled on the handle and crept inside.

MYSTERY AT MUSEUM. Police were called this morning to investigate a disturbance at the Museum of Ancient Thingamajigs. People in the neighbourhood reported a burglar alarm going off in the early hours, and a mysterious figure fleeing the scene. Museum director Dr Bernard Fossil was unavailable for comment…

CHAPTER ONE

AN UNIDENTIFIED
CHARGING
MONSTER

"HEEEEEELLLLLLLLLLLPPPPP
PPPP!!!!!!"someone yelled, but
they were drowned out by a spectacular
amount of noise and panic. People, busy

doing their shopping in the bustling market square, dived for safety.

Stalls were upturned, setting bowls of spices and towers of herbs flying through the air. Clouds of debris plumed everywhere.

Through all of this rampaged the source of the kerfuffle, with the deafening sound of stomping feet. The crowds parted as a strange beast galloped at full speed, darting wildly all over the place. It was covered in a becoming-grubbier-by-the-second white sheet so that no one knew what it was.

An elephant? No, too small.

A camel? No, although it was rather a strange shape.

A ferocious, unknown monster? It certainly seemed like it!

The creature hoofed in circles for several moments, collapsing a stall in on itself in the process and sending a wall of tightly rolled colourful carpets falling like dominos.

The beast charged again, this time directly into a stall hung with large golden teapots. One of the spouts caught hold of the sheet, throwing it to the ground so that finally the monster was visible for all to see.

Except it wasn't a monster.

It was a rather startled donkey, and on its back was the cause of all the palaver – a small, rather round penguin swinging round and round attached only by the handle of an umbrella.

"HEEEELLLLLP!" cried Mr Penguin, but before anyone could help, the donkey charged again and Mr Penguin found himself flying into the air. He landed with quite a heavy bump in a large basket, which tumbled and rolled for several seconds before coming to a stop.

Mr Penguin didn't dare open his eyes... a few shimmies of his shoulders had told him that he was surrounded by hundreds of thin, slithering objects.

"SNAKES!" cried Mr Penguin (not realising that he had fallen into a basket full of shoelaces) and with some terrific wiggling of the bottom he managed to clamber out, only to be walloped by the donkey again.

Back through the air Mr Penguin went, landing first with a BOING! on the stretched fabric roof of a stall selling olives, then skidding through a mountain of cinnamon before bouncing on the end of a large rolled-up carpet being carried by a rather alarmed-looking man. It catapulted him high above the market and directly into a date tree, where he swung around three times by the handle of his brolly before finally coming to a rather sticky sort of halt.

For a few moments there was a stunned silence as the market, now a complete mess, settled. Then a voice cried, "Mr Penguin?"

Mr Penguin opened his eyes, shoving his rather battered Adventuring hat off his face, and found that he was upside down and looking at the surprised face of a small boy wearing large glasses. There had been a cat sitting on his shoulder, but with all of Mr Penguin's rumpus, it had scarpered. The boy grinned up at Mr Penguin before shouting, "He's over here!"

Through the crowd came an elderly lady who, despite the ferocious heat, was wearing fifteen anoraks and had a pigeon on her head. She was accompanied by a large spider with a monobrow. Colin scribbled then held up his notepad.

It said:

COME DOWN HERE

Next page:

THIS INSTANT.

Mr Penguin, with the help of the small boy, struggled free (a shower of sticky dates rained down on him) and stood next to his friends, filthy and covered in, well, just about a little bit of everything from the market.

"Really, Mr Penguin!" said Edith Hedge, taking some birdseed from her pocket and offering it to Gordon, who refused it and concentrated on pecking at

her specs. "All this fuss because I wanted
a nice photograph of you next to that
donkey for my journal." From her bumbag
she pulled a crumpled old notebook and
an even more battered camera.

Mr Penguin sighed.

One minute he had been smiling
nicely for his picture and the next he'd just
popped his umbrella up to check it still
worked and it had startled the donkey.

What he really needed now was a
nice lie-down with a cold flannel on his
head, but there was no such luck. Edith
had her hands on her hips which meant
only one thing: she had an idea.

Colin was looking at Mr
Penguin with Pursed Lips.

He'd said all along that the umbrella was
a silly thing to bring to a hot, rainless
place like Laghaz. A parasol would have
been better, but Mr Penguin had insisted.
He liked to be prepared. It was like that
time he'd taken an electric fan when they
went to Cityville's indoor skiing centre.

"Now you know what I'm going
to say, don't you?" Edith said, and Mr
Penguin nodded.

"As my dear old mother used to
say," continued Edith, "if you make a
mess you have to…"

"Clean it up," said Mr Penguin,
feeling a bit warm about his bow tie as
he looked at the state of calamity all
around him.

Edith nodded, and handed a
broom to each of her friends.

Mr Penguin turned to say thank
you to the boy with the large spectacles

who had helped him down from the tree, but he'd vanished. So with a sigh, Mr Penguin straightened his hat, slid his umbrella into his satchel and started to tidy up with his friends.

←———•———→

The door to a small room above a busy café burst open. Two figures dashed in and ran straight to a desk. The room was so small that one of the inhabitants had to sit ON the desk, but actually they preferred it there. It gave them a better view.

Through the window, the hot, sandy city stretched out, full of life and noise. A palm tree rustled nearby and the breeze wafted through the mounds of papers on the desk, making a stubby red pencil clatter to the floor. The figure in the seat didn't look up. They were far too busy riffling through the papers. They peered intently through their large spectacles at the words and pictures on the pages before them, scanning through them and arranging them into piles.

Several of the sheets had photographs printed on them and had been clipped neatly from newspapers. Some of the articles were circled with the red pencil and marked with squiggly lines and exclamation marks.

The reader at the desk gathered these up, tapped them thoughtfully with a finger, then stuffed them into a notebook and put the book into a bag.

Then they found what they had come dashing into the room for, on a folded-up newspaper that had slipped off the desk in the excitement. They picked it up and read a small article at the bottom of the front page.

CELEBRATED ADVENTURERS ARRIVE IN TOWN TODAY

"*I knew it was him!*" *said the boy at the desk, pushing his spectacles up his nose.*

He circled the article with his red pencil and held it up for his companion to inspect.

The companion meowed loudly in agreement.

Very Interesting Indeed.

Then, taking the bag with the notebook in it with them, they bounded back out of the room.

CHAPTER TWO

A MYSTERY ON
THE DOORSTEP

Several hours later, and now even grubbier, Mr Penguin and his friends had finished their tidying and were settling into their hotel room.

They were, as Mr Penguin's very extravagant arrival through the market had announced, several thousand miles away from their home in Cityville. They were instead in the bustling city of Laghaz. It had been a very busy few months for the gang, who'd had a really ripping time solving lots of exciting mysteries. Rather than going straight back home, Edith had decided that they all needed a short break, and Colin, writing: NODDING VIGOROUSLY on his pad, had agreed.

Mr Penguin hadn't been too sure, and he still wasn't. The train journey to Laghaz had been very hot, and messing about in the market had made Mr Penguin hotter still, even with his jazzy new summer-weight bow tie and the special cooling lunchbox in his bag Edith had given him for his fish finger sandwiches.

He threw himself on to the hotel

bed and yawned loudly.

"I tell you what, why don't you and Colin stay here for a little while and rest?" said Edith. "Gordon and I can go and explore? It'll be cooler soon."

Mr Penguin thought this was a marvellous idea and, saying toodle-pip to Edith and Gordon, he and Colin got down to some serious relaxing. Mr Penguin clambered up on to the edge of the bathroom sink, plunged his feet (in their shoes) into some cold water and draped a moist flannel on his head.

AAH! Much better!

Colin settled himself on a pile of towels and pulled out the exciting book he and Mr Penguin were reading. It was all about spooky tombs, abandoned temples, haunted pyramids and, most thrilling of all, cursed mummies. It turned out that in the pyramids in this book there were always spooky dead pharaohs wrapped in bandages giving explorers the heebie-jeebies! Mr Penguin shuddered with excitement.

SHALL I READ? said Colin's notepad.

Mr Penguin nodded.

Colin cleared his throat by writing AHEM AHEM on his pad and began to read aloud.

Now, how Colin did this was quite interesting. First he read in his head, then immediately scribbled it down on to his pad before holding it up for Mr Penguin to read.

And – oh boy! – was the book thrilling!

For an hour the chums were engrossed in creepy tales from the crypt. They were just getting to a REALLY spooky bit when there was a sudden hammering on their door. They nearly leapt out of their skins.

They looked at each other.

Colin drew a ? on his pad and Mr Penguin agreed.

The hammering sounded again and Mr Penguin, quivering, wrapped himself up in a fluffy white bathrobe and padded damply to the door. He opened it a crack, feeling sure that outside would be a cursed mummy.

But there wasn't.

In the hallway outside was Edith.

"Hello!" said Mr Penguin.

And then something Very Strange happened.

Something Very Strange Indeed.

Edith said, "Excuse me, but you don't know where Edith is, do you?"

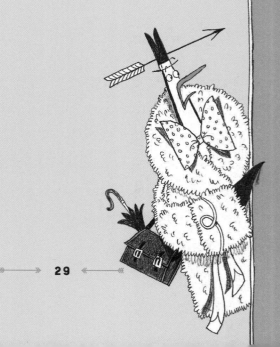

CHAPTER THREE

A FAMILIAR STRANGER

For two minutes there was utter confusion. Neither Mr Penguin or Edith really knew what was going on, or understood what the other was trying to explain.

Mr Penguin even started to wonder if HE was Edith.

Eventually Colin, calm as a cucumber as usual, clonked Mr Penguin on the ankle with his pen and took charge.

EXCUSE ME BUT WHAT EXACTLY IS GOING ON? said his pad.

PLEASE he added.

Edith twisted her handkerchief anxiously and explained. "I'm not Edith," she said. "My name is Cynthia Hedge and I am Edith's twin sister."

Mr Penguin gasped so ferociously his hat fell off. He whipped his magnifying glass out of his bag and had a good look at Cynthia. It became very clear that she wasn't Edith after all because firstly, she was wearing entirely different clothes and secondly, she didn't have a Gordon sitting on top of her head.

"I live here in Laghaz," continued

Cynthia, "and I was meant to be meeting Edith at a café, but she didn't arrive. You don't know where she is, do you?"

She looked so worried Mr Penguin couldn't help but feel the same. He'd had no idea Edith had a sister OR that she was meeting her. Had Edith got lost? he wondered. No, that wasn't like Edith at all. She ALWAYS knew where they were, and she was the one who always took charge of maps. (This was because the last time Mr Penguin was in charge of a map they'd all accidentally ended up inside the lion enclosure of a zoo.) Suddenly, Mr Penguin's stomach jumped a somersault. THERE WEREN'T ANY LIONS HERE, WERE THERE?

"Where were you meeting her?" he asked casually, trying to play it cool.

"Well," said Cynthia, "I write books and I often work in the library, so I said to meet me just around the corner from there."

Mr Penguin's worries disappeared instantly. He and Colin looked at each other and nodded. If there was one thing Edith couldn't resist, it was a library.

"I bet Edith snuck in there for a quick read and got distracted. She's ALWAYS in the Cityville library. Let's go and find her!" said Mr Penguin. He chucked off the bathrobe, checked his lunchbox and umbrella were in his bag and led Cynthia and Colin out of the hotel.

The market square was still very busy, even though the sun was beginning to set. Delicious smells filled the air, and as Mr Penguin followed Cynthia he had to work very hard to stop himself wandering off to dive into the cooking pots headfirst with his mouth open.

Eventually, they got to the large,

sandy-coloured library
building, decorated with
beautifully patterned tiles.
The two Adventurers and
Cynthia slipped inside.

But what they didn't know was that from the moment they had left the hotel, they were being watched. From the shadows, eyes peered at them through holes cut into newspapers.

As the Adventurers crossed the square the two onlookers had followed, creeping softly behind them and darting out of view every time Mr Penguin looked around.

As soon as Mr Penguin disappeared inside, the boy folded his holey newspaper away, pushed his specs up his nose and slipped into the library, followed on silent paws by his cat.

CHAPTER FOUR

SCATTERED
BIRDSEED

The vast book-lined rooms of the
library were wonderfully cool, and
Mr Penguin was tempted to lie belly-down
on the tiled floor, until he caught Colin
looking at him and shaking his head.

Although it was late in the afternoon, there were still a number of people wandering about with piles of books or dangling from tall ladders as they reached for thick tomes on teeteringly high shelves.

They all looked for Edith, but couldn't find her anywhere.

"I'll ask Professor Umlaut," said Cynthia, leading the way to an enormous desk heaped with paper and wobbling towers of books. "He's the librarian here and often helps me with my research."

She dinged a little bell.

From behind the clutter there was a startled squeak and a man's pink face appeared. There was something about his twitching nose and the way his hair stuck up like two long ears that remind Mr Penguin of a rabbit, and he wished he had a carrot to offer him.

"Oh! M-Miss Hedge!" stammered Professor Umlaut in a quiet voice. "I've been looking for that book for you, but I c-can't seem to put my hands on it…"

Cynthia told him not to worry and asked if he had seen Edith.

"That's her twin sister," said Mr Penguin, pleased to be able to help. "They are ABSOLUTELY identical except for not wearing the same clothes and being two different people."

Professor Umlaut said he hadn't seen anyone who looked like Cynthia, but then he had been quite busy that afternoon. He said he'd help them look for their friend, as he knew the library better than anyone.

They were glad of his help because the place was absolutely gigantic. The main reading room was vast and circular, with shelves on each

level reaching high into the domed roof.
Together, the gang searched all over
for Edith, but with no luck. She wasn't
in the Mechanical Engineering or Very
Complicated Science sections, or even the
teetering Pigeon Psychology Department.

"I'm afraid," said Professor Umlaut
in his quiet voice, "that your f-friend
doesn't seem to be here and—" But
before he could finish there came a loud
noise from the far side of the room.

It was a loud SQUAWKING noise.

GORDON! said Colin's pad.

Mr Penguin, Colin, Cynthia and
Professor Umlaut hoofed it towards the
sound. They tracked it down to a very
long, dark corridor with great swags of
cobwebs hanging between the
bookcases. A sign swung eerily
above their heads.

MYSTERY SECTION

Mr Penguin shivered.

Somewhere in the corridor, Gordon squawked again and – feeling Colin push him behind the knees – Mr Penguin began to run into the gloom. He didn't get very far when his foot slipped on something and he went flying, landing – CRASH! – into a mess of books. He blinked, straightened his bow tie and looked about. Among the books on the floor was… what? He picked a flipperful of it up and allowed it to tumble back to the ground.

Birdseed.

The exact same birdseed Edith kept in her pockets for Gordon to eat (except he much preferred to eat human food or things like socks and notepaper).

Mr Penguin squinted into the darkness around him. There was one thing for certain: Edith wasn't there.

But she had been.

By now Colin, Cynthia and Professor Umlaut had caught up with him. Colin dived into Mr Penguin's bag and emerged with the magnifying glass, which he used to inspect everything around them. There was some furious scribbling on his pad.

THERE HAS BEEN A KERFUFFLE HERE it said, and Mr Penguin agreed.

"But where's Gordon?" said Mr Penguin.

"Is that him?" asked Cynthia, pointing to a bookshelf above her head – and yes, there he was, shaking behind a book.

Mr Penguin clambered up and patted Gordon gently on the head, saying, "There! There!" and, "Stop trying to bite me" in a soothing voice. He tried to lift him down, but Gordon clamped his wings around a heavy book and wouldn't let go. The only way for Mr Penguin to rescue Gordon was to bring the book down with him. The book was called *Feeling Peckish? 1001 Recipes to Feed Your Pigeon* by someone called Paloma Aviary-Heron.

"What is this book doing in the mystery section?" asked Mr Penguin, but before he could think of an answer Colin tapped his friend on the ankle and held up his pad. He had drawn an arrow

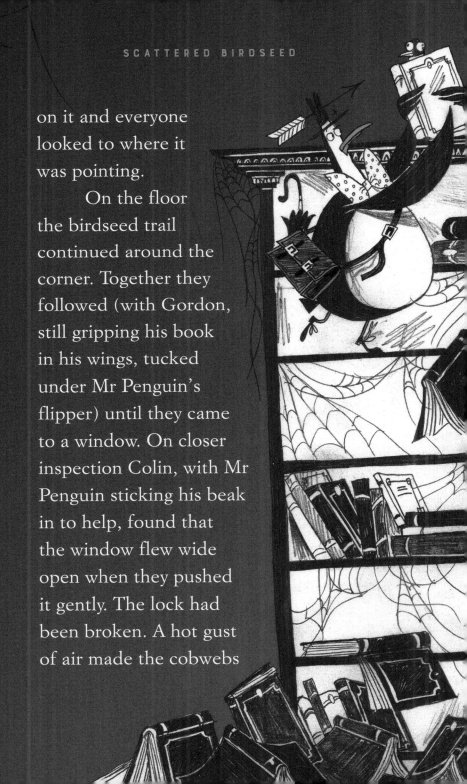

on it and everyone looked to where it was pointing.

On the floor the birdseed trail continued around the corner. Together they followed (with Gordon, still gripping his book in his wings, tucked under Mr Penguin's flipper) until they came to a window. On closer inspection Colin, with Mr Penguin sticking his beak in to help, found that the window flew wide open when they pushed it gently. The lock had been broken. A hot gust of air made the cobwebs

dance above their heads.

And it was then Mr Penguin discovered it: caught on the latch was a torn scrap of fabric.

"This has come from Edith's bumbag!" said Mr Penguin, holding it into the light.

Colin grabbed his pen and scribbled wildly on his pad before holding it up with a very stern look on his face.

I THINK EDITH HAS BEEN…

And he turned the page:

CHAPTER FIVE

KIDNAPPED

At this news, Mr Penguin thought about tumbling down into an extravagant faint, but before he could do so, Cynthia beat him to it. Well, she didn't faint, but sat down heavily and looked utterly flummoxed.

"Kidnapped?" she said hoarsely. "Edith?"

And Mr Penguin couldn't help but agree with her – it seemed so extraordinary. "Who on earth would kidnap Edith?" he whispered.

"Oh dear, oh dear!" twittered Professor Umlaut, looking a bit pale. "And in my library too... You don't suppose she just went out for some air, do you?"

Colin rolled his eyes under his monobrow.

OUT OF A WINDOW? said his pad.

"Oh yes, quite so... quite so..." said Professor Umlaut. "A fanciful i-i-idea."

Beside him, Cynthia was looking at the tumble of books and the spilt birdseed, piecing it all together.

"I suppose her kidnappers surprised her here and then bundled her up and carried her out of the window?" she said slowly.

Mr Penguin nodded. "She definitely wouldn't have left Gordon on his own unless someone sneaked up on her."

Mr Penguin knew this for certain. Every bit of him then started to quiver. He looked out of the window over the city of Laghaz. It was a sprawling jumble of sand-coloured buildings, peppered with palm trees and tall minarets. Edith could be ANYWHERE! he thought. How would they ever find her? In all his other adventures Mr Penguin had had his whole gang around him to help him solve crimes, and without Edith he felt very unsure where to start.

He decided to do what he usually did when he was unsure about things:

pretend. He clasped his flippers behind
his back and marched back and forth in
the manner of someone Very Clever.

"If only we had a clue," he mused,
but was interrupted by Gordon. The
pigeon started to make a strange noise.
It was a bit like a cat trying to bring up a
fur ball. It was only when Colin and Mr
Penguin looked very closely at him that
they realised their friend's cheeks
were all puffed out.

HE HAS SOMETHING
IN HIS GOB said Colin's pad.

Then, turning to
Gordon, Colin wrote:

DROP IT very firmly,
underlining it twice.

But Gordon wouldn't.

For several moments Mr Penguin
and Colin wrestled with Gordon, who
wouldn't release either the book he was

clinging to for safety OR what was in his mouth.

In the end Colin wrote:

KETCHUP BOTTLE HIM MR PENGUIN

Mr Penguin did as he was told. Upside down Gordon went, and Mr Penguin tapped his bottom lightly like he was trying to get the last bits of tomato

sauce out of the bottle.

Gordon clamped his beak shut for several moments, before eventually spitting out what he'd been trying to gobble. Mr Penguin gingerly picked it up from the floor.

It was a rather soggy piece of ripped and crumpled paper. The gang carefully smoothed it out and inspected it.

It was most definitely A Clue.

CHAPTER SIX

A DANGEROUS DESTINATION

Numbers.
A sheet of paper entirely covered in rows and rows of printed numbers, one set of which had been circled with a red pencil.

"Map coordinates?" said Professor Umlaut.

COMBINATION CODES FOR A SAFE? said Colin's pad.

"Telephone numbers for takeaway fish finger sandwich restaurants?" said Mr Penguin hopefully. He was feeling very anxious and, as always in those situations, his stomach was growling.

Colin gave him A Look and was just going to write something when Cynthia, who had been peering at the numbers very closely, picked up the piece of paper.

"No," she said. "None of those things. These are times, I'm sure of it. I... I think this is a train timetable."

She turned the paper over and yes – there, written at the top of the torn sheet was: LAGHAZ INTERNATIONAL TRAIN STA (The rest had been ripped off.)

"She didn't tell us about getting a train," said Mr Penguin, perplexed. It was very unlike Edith to keep secrets.

"Maybe her kidnappers were," said Cynthia.

Professor Umlaut looked at his watch.

"That train w-w… went quite a while ago now. And it looks like it was the last one t-t-today," he said. "I suppose if we went to the station they would be able to tell us where it goes?"

"I already know," said Cynthia, going all wobbly again. "Look!"

She showed the back of the paper to the gang and tapped it with a neatly painted nail. Printed on it was a section of a map crisscrossed with wiggling train lines. One destination was circled in the same red pencil.

Wadi al Khatar

"What does that mean?" said Mr Penguin. His flippers were shivering and his beak was starting to chatter.

"The Valley of Peril," whispered Professor Umlaut with a shudder. Mr Penguin gasped.

"A very spooky place," said Cynthia. "Full of abandoned temples, hidden crypts and," she gulped, "some of the tombs there are said to be guarded by ancient curses!"

And at this news Mr Penguin DID extravagantly faint.

He came to a moment later, just as Colin was going to bonk him on the head with a paperback. He lay for a few minutes with terrible thoughts bubbling in his mind: Edith quietly browsing for books, then a gang of fearsome bandits interrupting her. Edith trying to scarper but them bundling her up and squeezing out of the window. Edith tied up in a train speeding through the night.

The Valley of Peril... There was something about that place that Mr Penguin didn't like the sound of at all. It sounded like it might be quite perilous.

"We have to rescue Edith!" said Cynthia decisively, standing up. She had that determined look that Mr Penguin had seen from Edith many times.

"But the last train's gone," he said anxiously. "Perhaps if we just all go and sit nicely in the hotel with cold flannels on our heads until Edith returns? I expect she'll be back soon."

But even as he said it, he knew it was a silly thing to say. His friend was in danger. He HAD to find her.

"OK," he sighed. "How will we get There?" (He didn't dare say The Valley of Peril.)

Professor Umlaut looked at his watch again.

"Well," he said. "There is always the night train? It gets to the Valley early in the morning? Y-you'll have to be quick as it leaves in about ten minutes."

Everyone thought this was an excellent plan.

"You'd better come with us, Professor," said Cynthia. "We'll need all the help we can get if we are up against a troop of devious kidnappers!"

As Professor Umlaut bustled off to get his briefcase, Mr Penguin felt a tremble of nerves wiggle down his back. Being anywhere that wasn't his nice safe igloo office in Cityville always made him feel a bit wobbly about the knees, but he usually

had Edith with
him to be
reassuring. He
straightened his
hat and tried to be brave.

The gang all began to leave,
but Gordon wouldn't budge, clinging
to his book like glue. Mr Penguin tried
to prise it from him but Gordon
just clamped his beak tight and
tried to swallow it like he
was a python.

Eventually, with
much kerfuffling, Colin
managed to set the book
free and Mr Penguin
shoved it into his bag.

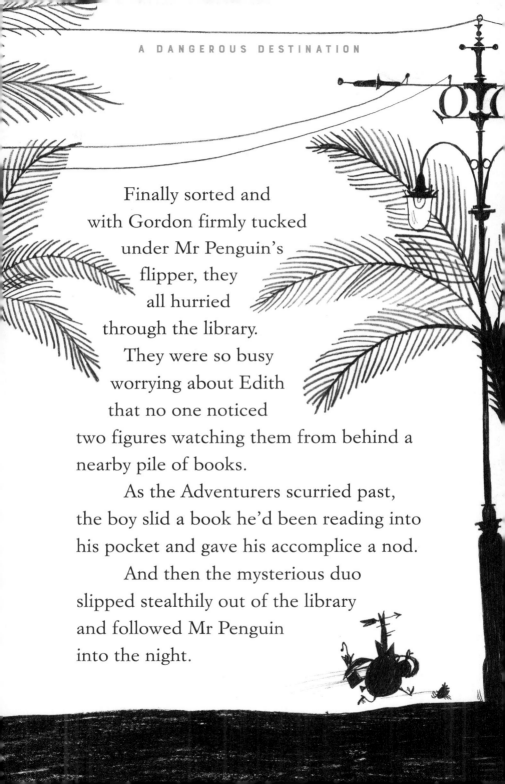

Finally sorted and
with Gordon firmly tucked
under Mr Penguin's
flipper, they
all hurried
through the library.
They were so busy
worrying about Edith
that no one noticed
two figures watching them from behind a
nearby pile of books.

As the Adventurers scurried past,
the boy slid a book he'd been reading into
his pocket and gave his accomplice a nod.

And then the mysterious duo
slipped stealthily out of the library
and followed Mr Penguin
into the night.

CHAPTER SEVEN

LIKE AN
ANGRY COBRA

The station was heaving. Great clouds of thick steam huffed from engines waiting to depart as the five Adventurers hoofed it to the ticket office. All around them, throngs of people bustled about, running for trains or selling things to passengers. Colin hastily made a thread of web from his bum and lassoed

Mr Penguin's ankle to stop his friend getting lost, or distracted by the smell of food.

Cynthia was as quick and as clever as Edith at Organising Things, and in an instant three first-class sleeper cabins had been booked for the gang on the exclusive night train.

They battled through the crowds and ran up the platform just as the conductor, very swankily dressed in an exquisite peacock-blue uniform, rang his bell.

"FINAL CALL FOR THE PYRAMID EXPRESS!" he cried, and Mr Penguin and chums quickly shuffled in behind a small queue of people waiting to board the gleaming first-class carriages.

Their fellow passengers all had suitcases and Mr Penguin felt a bit awkward with just his bag. He patted it for comfort, pleased to know that besides his

mummy book and the rather heavy book
Gordon seemed to have taken a shine to,
there was his umbrella and his nice new
lunchbox. It was keeping his sandwich
cool in the stifling heat.

That was just like Edith, he thought:
kind and practical. What she didn't have
in her bumbag wasn't worth having. Mr
Penguin hoped that wherever she was she
still had it with her and that the contents
would be helpful if she found herself in a
pickle.

As Mr Penguin stood at
the end of the line thinking
about Edith and

his packed lunch, he allowed himself to have a good look at his fellow passengers. Leaning around a rather tall man with an extraordinary amount of cases, Mr Penguin watched a grand, elderly woman being heaved on board by the train stewards. Behind her, a squirrelish sort of woman fussed with a mass of hat boxes. Then there was a man with a pair of glasses clipped to his nose and the letters B.F. in gold on his case. Behind him, a tiny man with an egg-shaped head and an extravagant moustache flicked through a book by someone called Ms Christie.

Next to Mr Penguin, Colin flexed his kung fu kicking legs, Professor Umlaut was reading a book and Cynthia twisted her handkerchief.

Poor Cynthia, thought Mr Penguin, she looked frightfully worried.

The line shortened, but as Mr Penguin got ready to follow Colin up the steps he caught his breath. He'd suddenly had a very strange sensation. It was like someone had put an ice cube under his hat and allowed it to slide right down to his shoelaces. Despite the heat of the station, Mr Penguin shivered. He felt like he was being watched... but by whom?

He looked around to see that the platform was now practically empty. There were a few smartly dressed train stewards faffing about with the final pieces of

luggage, but no one was eyeballing him.
And yet he still felt that sensation of eyes
on him.

Was there someone peering at him
from a shadowy corner?

Had he heard footsteps?

He gasped. Was he being followed by
a cursed mummy? He was heading to the
Valley of Peril, after all. Maybe a long-dead
pharaoh was going too?

He felt himself starting to do his
panicky dance, when something poked him
in the belly and he yelped.

"AAARGH!"

Oh! It was only Colin.

HURRY UP YOU PLONKER! said
the pad, and with a final glance at the
empty platform Mr Penguin hoisted
himself aboard.

The train was magnificent. The
wood-panelled walls were so well polished

Mr Penguin could see his rather sweaty reflection in them. Tiny lamps glowed cosily and the brass fittings gleamed in the light.

It was a bit of a tight squeeze in the corridor and at the front of the carriage an important-looking train steward was fussing with a clipboard and allocating everyone their berths.

The elderly woman (a princess!) took quite a bit of time to get settled, mainly because her hat was so enormous she got wedged in the doorway for several minutes because she refused to take it off.

With a huff and a great puffing of steam, the train left the station and slowly the entire carriage began to rock.

The conductor appeared to announce that the dining car would be open in an hour for dinner, and Mr Penguin's eyes gleamed.

Food!

On the train!

He leant forward to tap Colin on the head to make sure he had heard the good news, when the train suddenly lurched and stopped sharply with a screech of brakes.

After a bit of shouting from the engine end of things it started up again. As it did, Mr Penguin lost his footing and – OOOF! – he and Gordon bounced down the corridor, ricocheting off the walls. He walloped into the tall man with all the luggage from

earlier, and several of the gentleman's cases crashed to the floor.

Mr Penguin lay blinking for a moment then sat up and straightened his hat.

"I say," said the tall man in a polite, quiet voice. "Are you OK, old bean?"

Mr Penguin didn't answer immediately because, peeking through the jumble of cases, he'd caught sight of something that made his flippers go all goose-pimply.

"I said, are you OK?" the tall man repeated, a little louder.

Mr Penguin pulled himself together.

He realised that he had been peering between the tall man's legs like they were a window.

Mr Penguin nodded and apologised in his nice telephone voice.

"Don't worry about it," said the man, and very kindly he straightened Mr Penguin's bow tie for him, before gathering his cases, quietly slipping into his cabin and closing the door.

Mr Penguin's flippers were still all of a fumble at what he'd seen: he'd spotted one of the other passengers – the elderly man with B.F. on his suitcase – about to enter his cabin, but with the commotion of Mr Penguin flying through the air he'd stopped, startled. It was then that B.F. had caught sight of another of the train's passengers and his face had darkened. He'd looked as angry as a cobra about to strike. But who had he been looking at to cause such a reaction?

Mr Penguin stared down the corridor, but the only person there was timid Professor Umlaut, letting himself into his cabin with his nose still stuck in his book.

B.F. went into his own room and slammed the door.

Mr Penguin dusted Gordon off and they followed Colin into their cabin.

He wasn't quite sure why, but he found himself shivering for the second time in five minutes.

OOF! That was close!

Two shadowy figures sat panting in the crowded baggage car of the Pyramid Express.

They had very nearly missed the train! A lucky screech of brakes and they'd hurled themselves on board.

There was no time to catch their breath, though. They had work to do.

So the boy and the cat picked themselves up and set out to find what they were looking for...

Two Months Earlier:

It was well past midnight, but none of the fancy people sitting at tables in the Birdcage Cabaret Theatre were in their pyjamas or even thinking about going to bed.

They glittered in their snazziest clothes, sparkled with jewels and were having the most marvellous time as jazz hooted and glasses clinked.

Through the audience, sequins gleaming in the spotlight, slunk an incredibly glamorous blonde woman on towering heels. She was dripping in jewels: dangling diamond earrings, an enormous necklace, arms full of bangles. As she moved she jangled like a very expensive wind chime.

Gratefully taking the hand of an admirer, she stepped lightly on to the stage and finished the final few bars of the very jazzy song she'd been singing. The room erupted. Cries of "More!" filled the air, but the woman curtsied gracefully, gathered her feather boa about her shoulders and exited stage right.

Backstage, the Birdcage Cabaret Theatre was a very different affair. It was dark, dusty and incredibly cramped. The woman had to squeeze against the wall to allow a troupe of dancers bedecked in feathers to cancan their way on to the stage. Eventually, she made it back to her dressing room. It was the biggest one, with a large golden star announcing who she was:

Miss Precious Darling

Miss Darling locked the door behind

her and sat down wearily in front of the mirror. All around it bright light bulbs shone on her heavily made-up face. The room was a tip. A rail of frothy costumes, shoes tossed into a pile, a bin overflowing with lipstick-stained blotting papers and face powder everywhere.

But Miss Darling didn't notice the mess. It was late and she was hurrying to leave.

She started by removing her jewellery. Off came the bangles and bracelets. The earrings were plucked from her ears and she began decanting her gems carelessly into a velvet bag she had taken from her large handbag. Anyone watching would have marvelled at the sheer amount of it all. Strangely, there seemed to be more going into the bag than she had been wearing.

Finally, she slipped the necklace over her beautifully coiffed hair and ran the chain through her fingers. Hanging from the end of it was a large, heavy, triangular amulet. It was

solid gold and studded with more jewels
than you could count. She pulled a tissue
from her dress and was polishing it when
there was a knock at the door.

"There is someone here to see you,
Miss Darling," came a voice.

"Can't they wait?" she said.

"Um… I'm afraid they said it was

rather urgent," said the voice, nervously.

Sighing, Miss Darling put the necklace down on her dressing table, hid it with a chiffon scarf, threw on a maribu-edged peignoir and left the room.

Silence.

Stillness.

Then, from a hiding place behind the costume rack, a figure emerged. They reached out, snatched the necklace and slipped it into a bag. And then they left.

You see, that's the thing about the backstage of a theatre: it's always busy and has so many dark corners to hide in. And that is why nobody noticed a stranger sneaking from the dressing room, merging with the shadows before slipping out of the stage door.

They snuck right past Miss Darling and she didn't see a thing.

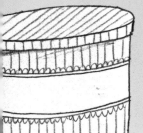

MYSTERIOUS GOINGS-ON AT THE BIRDCAGE THEATRE. Police are asking for assistance to help solve a mystery at a popular local cabaret theatre.

Last night, following a performance, stage sensation Miss Precious Darling vanished without trace.

Stranger still, several items have been reported missing by members of the audience.

CHAPTER EIGHT

STEALING JIGSAWS

Mr Penguin's cabin was magnificent, but his nerves were in too much of a jangle for him to really appreciate the plump-pillowed, crisp-sheeted loveliness of it all.

As soon as the door was closed, Mr Penguin, talking in Hushed Tones, filled Colin in on everything that had just happened: the angry look from B.F., the feeling of being watched, his worries about being pursued by an ancient cursed mummy.

Colin listened intently, waggling his eyebrows with interest and holding up ! and ? on his notepad at exactly the right dramatic moments. If he'd put his mind to it, Mr Penguin could have worked himself up into quite a tizz, but Colin, as always, came to the rescue. On each of the neatly made bunk beds in the room there was a collection of chocolate truffles. Colin handed them to Mr Penguin, who swallowed them down one after the other. By the last one he even managed to unwrap the chocolate first.

"Much better!" he sighed.

But what were they going to do?

Colin leapt into action.

Humming the very exciting action song he sang whenever he was Up To Something, Colin hopped off the bed, scuttled to the door and peered around it suspiciously. Then he disappeared. A moment later he was back, waggling a sheet of paper from one of his arm-legs. He'd borrowed it from the carriage steward's clipboard.

Whilst Gordon, besotted with Mr Penguin's satchel, pecked happily at it, Mr Penguin and Colin examined the paper. It was a list of who was in each cabin.

THE PYRAMID EXPRESS FIRST—
CLASS SLEEPER CARRIAGE:

CABIN 1: Cynthia Hedge
CABIN 2: Professor Earnest Umlaut
CABIN 3: Mr Penguin, Colin
   and Gordon
CABIN 4: Mr U. Bland
CABIN 5: Dr B. Fossil
CABIN 6: Princess Anastasia Borscht
CABIN 7: Ms Greta Schmidt
CABIN 8: M. Hercules Parrot

Mr Penguin carefully matched up the
names with the people who had been
queuing on the platform. Princess
Anastasia was the elderly lady with the
large hat and Ms Schmidt was her

assistant. Mr Bland was the quiet man next door so Dr Fossil must be the man with B.F. on his case, meaning that the man with the egg-shaped head and the twirly moustache was Monsieur Parrot.

"Why was Dr Fossil so angry?" asked Mr Penguin. It had been jolly warm in the corridor so perhaps he was feeling a bit sweaty? Mr Penguin considered then shook his head. No, the heat was annoying, but Dr Fossil had been SEETHING with anger like a hissing cat.

Colin straightened his monobrow determinedly.

WE WILL KEEP AN EYE ON HIM AT DINNER said his pad.

Colin yawned.

I THINK WE SHOULD REST NOW BECAUSE WE HAVE BEEN VERY

Next page: BUSY.

And with that, he flipped himself upside down and immediately fell asleep, snoring and flexing his kung fu kicking legs.

Mr Penguin sat quietly in the unlit cabin. Outside, the bright lights of Laghaz had disappeared and been replaced by the inky, star-spangled desert sky.

His thoughts turned to Edith. She was somewhere out there, but where? And why would anyone kidnap her? And was he even looking for her in the right place?

Hmm. That WAS a worrying thought. The only clue they had was a chewed-up train timetable. Did that even belong to Edith's kidnappers? Gordon ate anything, so he might have found it anywhere.

"I mean, look!" said Mr Penguin to himself. "He's trying to eat my satchel!"

He sighed. Edith would know what

to do, he thought. Edith was clever and had taught him so many useful things. "Be brave, Mr Penguin!" she'd say. "Use your brain, Mr Penguin." "No, Mr Penguin, gluing your hat to your head to stop it flying off in the wind isn't very clever" – all of this excellent advice.

He sighed again. He didn't like not having all his friends around him. Together they made an excellent team: Colin was the king of kung fu, Edith was clever and even Gordon seemed to have a giant heap of secret skills. Then a not-very-jolly thought crossed his mind.

"What am I good at?" harrumphed Mr Penguin. He had the sneaking suspicion that without all his friends around him the only thing he WAS good at was eating fish finger sandwiches.

His belly rumbled. The late dinner service didn't begin until 9 p.m., so there was still an hour to go. Perhaps he could just have the teeniest, tiniest nibble of one of his sandwiches? He tried to take his lunchbox out of his bag, but Gordon was pecking at it like mad and caused such a kerfuffle that he had to stop and wrestle Gordon under his flipper. He patted him on the head soothingly until he calmed down. What HAD got into him? wondered Mr Penguin. Probably missing Edith.

Cool late-evening air drifted through the window, and as he sat on the bed, swaying slightly as the train chugged through the night, Mr Penguin's eyelids started to droop. He forgot about eating and with a yawn fell into a strange snoring kind of a doze.

It wasn't a good nap. Mr Penguin's brain quivered like jelly with worrying thoughts. One moment he imagined

scenes of Edith's kidnapping, next
glowing eyes watched him from the
darkness, then he was back on that
donkey charging about the market being
chased by the spooky mummies from his
and Colin's book.

Suddenly, the train jolted.
Everything in the cabin jumped. Gordon
slipped from Mr Penguin's flippers and
clattered to the floor, knotting himself up
in the strap of Mr Penguin's bag.

"What's happening?" Mr Penguin
cried.

Groggy and only half-awake, he slid
off the bed to rescue Gordon – and as he
did, he heard something. Someone was
talking in another cabin, and their not
very nice-sounding words were being
carried to Mr Penguin through the open
window.

"We are so close!" the voice hissed.

"We just need the final piece of the jigsaw
– I know it's on this train. And I will find
it – even if I have to steal it!"

Mr Penguin froze. Puzzles? Stealing?
On the train?

He gasped. BANDITS!

He padded softly towards the
window, straining to listen, and that's
when he saw it.

There! Right in front of him,
looming out of the darkness outside the
window: a face!

A terrible, not-human face.

And it was glaring at him with one,
glowing eye.

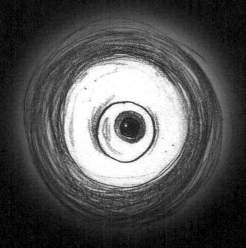

CHAPTER NINE

SUDDEN
DARKNESS

S everal things happened one after the other.

Firstly, Mr Penguin stumbled backwards and found himself wedged, bum to the ceiling, in a cupboard.

Then, startled awake, Colin leapt
into action again. With sleep-heavy eyes he
charged about the room kung fu kicking
and dancing about with his fists up ready
to biff anyone on the nose, his pad
bobbing about with: FISTICUFFS IS IT?
Not finding anyone, he KAPOW-ed the
light switch and the cabin filled with light.

He hauled Mr Penguin out of the
cupboard and watched as his friend ran
about, panicking, the arrow poking
through his hat quivering like mad.

WHAT ON EARTH said Colin's
pad, adding ??????? to show his
confusion.

Mr Penguin started to yell: "A
GHOST! A CURSED MUMMY! A FACE
AT THE WINDOW!"

Colin jumped to investigate, but
there was nothing there. Just the desert
streaming past under a wide moonlit sky.

There was a knock at the door and had Colin not caught him, Mr Penguin would have jumped back into the cupboard.

It was Cynthia, looking concerned.

"Is everything OK?" she asked.

HE'S HAD A BAD DREAM said Colin's pad.

Cynthia made soothing sorts of noises and after a moment Mr Penguin pulled himself together. Yes, he thought, it must have been a dream, but the face had certainly seemed VERY real.

"I'm terribly worried about Edith," said Cynthia, fussing with her handbag, "but I suppose we ought to eat something? Would some dinner make you feel better? It's gone nine now so the dining car is open."

Mr Penguin nodded. Leaving Gordon to snooze in the room (promising to bring him a doggy bag later), Colin and Mr Penguin followed Cynthia and Professor Umlaut down the corridor.

The restaurant carriage was Most Splendid. Waiters, smart in their white jackets and black dickies, fluttered about between the tables. Princess Anastasia (in a different giant hat now) was chomping away as her companion, Ms Schmidt, twittered beside her. Monsieur Parrot was engrossed in his book, and Dr Fossil had his nose firmly in the menu.

Mr Penguin eyeballed the doctor as he waddled past his table. There was no trace of the angry cobra look on his face now. He just seemed like a normal gentleman trying to decide what to eat.

Cynthia and Professor Umlaut were very nice and chattered away all through the courses. Cynthia explained about the books she wrote. They weren't exciting stories with penguins in them

(Mr Penguin was disappointed) but clever-sounding books with facts all about people a long time ago like the pharaohs. Her work had taken her all over the world but she'd settled in Laghaz to be close to the excellent library there. Professor Umlaut nattered merrily between mouthfuls of tagine and fluffy couscous.

Mr Penguin tried his hardest to listen politely but inside he was still all of a flutter. He was so jittery he was finding it hard to eat, so he could only manage five or six helpings of everything on the menu. His awful dreams and the face at the window were fresh in his mind, as were those words he'd overheard. Who had spoken them? What had they said? Something about stealing a – what was it? A jigsaw!

Funny thing to steal, thought Mr Penguin, and shuddered. So there were

BANDITS on the train...

"I've ALWAYS been interested in history," Cynthia was saying. "Edith and I used to join Father and Mother on trips when we were girls. They were archaeologists. I've got a picture, let me show you." She ferreted about in her handbag for a moment and pulled out a very old photo. It was of two smiling girls and their parents, surrounded by other children.

Mr Penguin and Colin only vaguely took it in as their eyes flicked to the end of the carriage. Mr Bland had arrived, gracefully following the waiter to a table near the door.

At that moment Mr Penguin's table were presented with dessert menus, which they all studied very carefully. Suddenly, Mr Penguin found himself poked in the belly with a breadstick, and a sheet of Colin's notepaper was slid surreptitiously in front of his beak behind the menu.

AHEM it said.

Mr Penguin's eyes slid to Colin, who was hiding behind his own menu. He held up a picture of an arrow. Mr Penguin's eyes followed it. It was pointing at Dr Fossil.

Mr Penguin gasped. The doctor was spying – actually spying – from behind his menu at the back of Professor Umlaut's

head and, more worryingly, the angry
cobra look was back. His moustache was
bristling like a furious caterpillar.

Professor Umlaut didn't seem to
notice – he and Cynthia were still
nattering happily – but words swam about
in Mr Penguin's mind. KIDNAPPERS!
BANDITS! CURSED MUMMIES!
ONE-EYED FACE!

His flippers started to tremble.

Then, all of a sudden:

POP!

PPPFF!

All the lights in the carriage went
out, and the train was plunged into
darkness.

CHAPTER TEN

DON'T PANIC!
(PANIC!)

For a moment Mr Penguin wondered whether it really was pitch black or if he had just closed his eyes very tightly and forgotten to open them again. He patted his face to check. No, his eyes were open and the carriage really was in darkness. Then the pandemonium started.

Colin fumbled for his notepad and pen, wrote DON'T PANIC and held it up, but it was useless. Nobody could see anything, so they DID panic, and no one more so than Mr Penguin.

He pushed back his seat and began waddling up and down the carriage, crashing into everyone and everything. He was soon joined by others. Diners and waiters bumbled this way and that, plates slid from tables and smashed on the floor, and everyone was yelling in confusion.

Suddenly, Mr Penguin had the familiar feeling of one of Colin's webs lassoing him around the ankle. It stopped him in his tracks, mainly because it made him fall flat on his face, then dragged him backwards under the table.

There was a rough sort of scraping sound. A match flickered into life. In its glow, Colin lit a candle and the two

Adventurers looked at each other.

Out came Colin's pad.

STAY HERE it said.

Next page:

I MEAN IT.

And he dived off into the darkness
to see if he could find the light switch and
fix it.

Mr Penguin sat all of a jitter under
the table in the dim light of the candle.

He carefully lifted the tablecloth to get a
better view and saw feet dashing about.
The candlelight wasn't very strong, but in
the murky glow he saw Cynthia and
Professor Umlaut's legs shuffling about
looking for a seat, and there was the
elderly Princess Anastasia with her glittery
frock hitched up showing her bloomers,
galloping about in a panic and pursued by
Ms Schmidt yelling at her to calm down.

There was a noise behind him and Mr Penguin spun around, expecting to see Colin.

But it wasn't Colin.

Mr Penguin found himself looking once again into the single glowing yellow eye of the face that had been at the window earlier.

Mr Penguin screamed, stood up (whacking his head on the table) and stumbled out into the carriage.

"G... G... GHOST!" he yelled, and in his panic he managed to hurl the lit candle accidentally into a jug of water, extinguishing it with a fizz. The dining car was in darkness again, but then, after a moment – PING! – the lamps lit again.

Everyone blinked.

Mr Penguin looked around, his heart thumping in his chest like a marching band drum. Everyone was there, albeit rather dishevelled and a bit embarrassed.

There were Cynthia and Professor Umlaut, sitting at a table with their eyes like saucers.

There was Dr Fossil, looking rather surprised at finding Princess Anastasia on his lap.

Ms Schmidt was at the other end of the carriage, pink-faced because she had mistakenly captured a waiter in a tablecloth, thinking it was the princess.

And there, sitting at his same seat, was Mr Bland, his hair flopping down and his dickie-bow crooked.

The only person not flustered was Monsieur Parrot, who was still in his seat looking unmoved. He simply screwed his monocle back into his eye and continued turning the pages of his book.

Colin scuttled over to Mr Penguin.

SOMEONE HAD CUT THE ELECTRIC CABLE said his pad.

BUT I FIXED IT WITH SOME WEB.

He turned the page.

FROM MY BUM.

"Why would anyone cut the lights?" panted Mr Penguin, still ruffled from seeing that face again in the gloom, but before Colin could answer there came the foghorn-sounding squawk of Gordon from the sleeper carriage. It was a dreadful noise, like an alarm going off.

"GORDON!" cried Mr Penguin, and everyone raced to find him.

At the door of the sleeper compartment, Colin stopped abruptly and held up one of his leg-arms. Everyone halted and watched as he surveyed the scene suspiciously from under his monobrow.

THE CABIN DOORS ARE AJAR
said his pad.

"What jars?" whispered Mr
Penguin. He vaguely hoped that if there
were some jars about, they might have
fish paste in them.

NO AJAR MEANS THEY ARE
ALL OPEN A BIT said Colin, pointing.
And he was right – every cabin door was
ever so slightly open. The passengers
watched with their breath held as Colin
crept down the corridor, kicking open
each door and looking inside. He scuttled
back and wrote two words on his pad.

RANSACKED he said.

And on the next page:

BANDITS.

CHAPTER ELEVEN

A HIDEYHOLE

The Pyramid Express started up again fairly quickly, but it took well over an hour for any sort of calm to return to the first-class sleeper carriage.

Colin, assisted by the train conductor and a very nervous Mr Penguin, inspected each cabin in turn and found that he had been correct. Every one of them had been broken into and every case, cupboard and bag had been rummaged through… but nothing had been taken.

VERY ODD.

Afterwards everyone tidied up and at almost midnight they settled themselves down for the night. There had been an additional brief moment of panic when Mr Penguin discovered a terrifying insect on him, only for Colin to inspect it closely and discover that it was, in fact, a large false eyelash. Where had THAT come from? Colin gave Mr Penguin a paper bag to breathe into and made him lie on the bunk bed with his legs in the air.

Mr Penguin felt better after that.

It was now almost one in the morning. Everyone was asleep except the inhabitants of Cabin 3. Huddled together, Colin, Mr Penguin and, to a lesser extent, Gordon were going through the events of the evening. There were so many questions to answer, but Mr Penguin was alternating between gnawing on the end of his flipper, and whispering in a trembling voice about bandits and the face he'd seen in the darkness.

Colin had to poke him in the belly with his pen to calm him down. Then he wrote (smaller than usual because he was whispering):

LET'S GET ORGANISED.

Next page:

FACTS:

1. SOMETHING STRANGE IS DEFINITELY GOING ON. BUT WHAT?

2. WHO HAS KIDNAPPED EDITH AND WHY?

3. WHERE IS EDITH?

4. WHY DID DR FOSSIL LOOK SO ANGRY WITH PROFESSOR UMLAUT?

5. WHY WAS DR FOSSIL SPYING ON PROFESSOR UMLAUT?

6. WHO CUT THE ELECTRICITY CABLE?

7. WHO RANSACKED THE CABINS AND WHY WAS NOTHING TAKEN?

8. THERE IS DEFINITELY A THIEF ON THE TRAIN BUT WHAT DO THEY WANT TO STEAL?

Mr Penguin took the pen and wrote an extra question:

> 9. Why is Mr Penguin being followed by the spooky face of a cursed mummy?

He shuddered again at the memory of that single glowing eye and the strange almost shrunken face.

Together the Adventurers looked at the list and scratched their heads. It really was perplexing. It was like someone had emptied out a box of jigsaw pieces, but then hidden the box so that they didn't

know what picture they were trying to
make. The pieces fitted together, but
how?

Hang on! thought Mr Penguin.
"JIGSAWS!" he cried.

He'd heard that voice say something
just before he saw the spooky face for the
first time. Something about jigsaws and
stealing…

"How do jigsaws fit into all of this?"
he asked, but neither he nor Colin knew.

He sighed and wished again that
Edith were there. One of the many things
she was clever at was spotting clues when
you didn't think there were any. She saw
codes and ideas in things when everyone
else just saw a big muddle. Mr Penguin
could absolutely only see confusion at the
moment.

Worrying about Edith made his
belly rumble anxiously. There was nothing

else for it. He HAD to have his fish finger sandwich.

Trying not to wake Gordon who was upside down, snoring, Mr Penguin carefully undid the straps of his satchel and rummaged inside for his lunchbox. It was a bit tricky because as well as his lunch there were two books in there, his magnifying glass, an umbrella, quite a large quantity of sand and several very sticky dates from the market earlier.

He wasn't quite careful enough with his rummaging though, and before he knew it, Gordon's eyes had pinged open and he'd launched himself at the open bag.

"What's got into him?" Mr Penguin asked Colin, who was holding Gordon back by the ankle.

Colin shrugged, accidentally let go of Gordon, and the pigeon hurled himself at the bag again. Both bird and bag clattered across the room and everything fell to the floor with a great number of thuds.

The room was a mess and in the middle of it, Gordon was dancing about happily. Colin went to rescue him, and that's when he saw it:

The book Gordon had clung to in the library and insisted on bringing with them was wide open, and the pages inside had been hollowed out to make a hideyhole.

And hidden there were some sheets of paper.

Colin inspected them closely. THESE HAVE BEEN TORN FROM EDITH'S JOURNAL said his pad.

Trembling, Mr Penguin absent-mindedly scooped up his fish finger sandwich from the floor and bit into it.

Instead of biting into the usual delicious fishfingeriness, his beak chomped on to something very hard indeed.

He pulled it from his mouth and they all looked at it.

There, hanging from a bejewelled chain, was a large triangular amulet. It was solid gold and studded with more jewels than you could count. It was undoubtedly very beautiful, but the way the jewels gleamed in the moonlight made Mr Penguin think of that spooky face in the window.

They appeared from the shadows and looked around.

They'd have to try again, that was for certain. Their task was Very Important.

They were definitely in the right carriage. They knew that because they'd been there earlier but had had to scarper pretty quickly.

The two strangers crept into the sleeper car and began to tiptoe around the steward, who was fast asleep in her chair. The figures moved almost silently, but not quite silently enough. With a sudden snort, the steward's eyes flickered open. She glanced sleepily around.

Huh! There was nothing there.

In the shadows where they had hidden, the two figures held their breath.

The steward looked at her pocket watch, heaved herself wearily out of her chair and shuffled away into the next carriage.

In the darkness, the two strangers felt their hearts thumping. That had been another close call.

The three eyes they had between them were wide with alarm.

CHAPTER TWELVE

A VERY EXPENSIVE SANDWICH

F or a moment, Mr Penguin and Colin
didn't say anything, they just stood
looking at each other. The necklace
dangled from Mr Penguin's flipper.

"This is an unusual fish finger," said Mr
Penguin, and Colin clipped him around
the ankle for being so silly.

IT'S AN AMULET said his pad
AND AN ANCIENT AND VERY
EXPENSIVE ONE TOO.

He examined it closely.

"AN ANCIENT AND VERY
EXPENSIVE AMULET?" exclaimed Mr
Penguin loudly, before clamping his
flippers over his mouth. "What's it doing
in my nice sandwich?" he whispered.

Colin didn't know.

"Does it belong to Edith?" hissed
Mr Penguin. It must, because who else
would have put it in his lunchbox? But
where did she get it from? And what was
she doing hiding things in his sandwiches?

Unless, thought Mr Penguin, this
amulet is actually made out of chocolate?
He carefully tried nibbling a bit. No –

definitely solid gold.

Colin busied himself by spreading the hidden papers out on the bed and the two chums peered at them closely, sharing the magnifying glass as they did so. They were definitely Edith's – her handwriting was scattered all over them. There were pages of hard-to-read notes and numbers and codes. What did it all mean?

There were other things too: newspaper clippings mainly.

There was one from three months ago about an incident at the Museum of Ancient Thingamajigs. It said the museum director Dr Fossil had been unavailable for comment.

"DR FOSSIL!" cried Mr Penguin.

Colin SSSSH-d him on his pad.

There was another clipping, this time from two months ago. Someone called Miss Precious Darling had been performing at a theatre, then she'd disappeared.

Colin shifted through the papers and found several photos.

First, there was a series of pictures cut from magazines. One was of the famous country music singer Hank Banjo, the next Miss Precious Darling, looking glamorous with her long eyelashes and her big, lipsticky smile. Then there was a picture of a serious-looking man called Cuthbert Verb, who was a famous writer.

On each picture Edith had drawn a large question mark.

After that, Colin found a copy of the picture Cynthia had shown them at dinner of her and Edith as children at a party with their parents and friends. Mr Penguin looked at Edith's wide, smiling grin and couldn't help but smile himself.

Finally there was a scrap of paper on which two mysterious words were written in Edith's handwriting.

JASPER CHARADE.

Colin looked at everything spread out on the bunk bed.

EDITH WAS INVESTIGATING SOMETHING said his pad.

Next page:

BUT WHAT?

Finally, Colin smoothed out a sheet of paper which revealed itself to be a map. It was very similar to the one on the back of the train timetable earlier. The two Adventurers studied it closely. There was a cross drawn on it with a red pencil. The Valley of Peril.

HMMM… said Colin's pad.

SO WE ARE GOING TO THE RIGHT PLACE.

Mr Penguin started to waddle about in a panic again. First Edith was kidnapped, then a spooky, one-eyed face was haunting him, then a robbery on the train and now this: a lot of evidence gathered by Edith, but evidence of what?

And, of course, the amulet. He looked at it. It was obviously priceless, and Edith had wanted it kept safe.

"What should we do?" hissed Mr Penguin.

Colin considered for a moment, but that moment was too long for Mr Penguin. He suddenly had a ping of inspiration. Edith was always telling him to use his brain and his brain was telling him they were in danger. They had to tell someone.

He gathered up his things, stuffed them back in his bag and slung it over his shoulder. He scooped Gordon up in one flipper and Edith's papers and the amulet in the other.

WHERE ARE YOU GOING? said Colin's pad. IT'S MIDNIGHT!

"We need help with all of this!" said Mr Penguin, and the three Adventurers set out down the corridor. It was dimly lit and empty. For the briefest of moments Mr Penguin thought he heard something move in the gloom, but he dismissed it.

He and Colin tiptoed down the hall and knocked on Professor Umlaut's and Cynthia's doors. There was a pause and Mr Penguin noticed that he was goose-pimpled again.

Then Professor Umlaut and Cynthia appeared, both looking half asleep.

"H-h-hello?" said Professor Umlaut.

"Mr Penguin? Is everything OK?" yawned Cynthia.

Mr Penguin held up the amulet and the papers and was just about to start explaining when from down the hall there came the thundering of feet.

In a split second, a great many things happened.

Someone was suddenly upon Mr Penguin and his pals. There was a confusion of sights and sounds:

Cynthia cried out in surprise, Professor Umlaut gasped, Colin kung fu kicked with all his might – but it was no good.

The amulet and papers were snatched from Mr Penguin's flippers. He was lifted into the air and tossed into a scratchy sack. Colin and Gordon were chucked in with him.

And then, to Mr Penguin's complete surprise, he found that he and his friends were hurled, like a bag of garbage, out of the speeding train.

Earlier that day:

The late-afternoon crowds were still bustling about the

*market in Laghaz. Near the library,
under a tall, shady palm tree, a figure leant
against the cool tiled wall. For anyone
watching them (and nobody was) there
wasn't anything suspicious about them at all.*

*But, if an observer had looked more
closely, they'd have seen that their eyes were
darting greedily about, scanning the people
as they hurried by.*

And there she was!

*The person they were looking for: an
elderly woman in fifteen anoraks, cinched at
the waist with a large bumbag, and a pigeon
perched peacefully on her head. The woman
was walking rather quickly, but seeing the
library building, she stopped. This was
obviously where she wanted to be, so she
hurried inside.*

*From the shadows, unwatched, the
figure slipped in behind her. If anyone had
seen them, they would have seen quite a*

devious smile stretched across their face.

But, of course, no one was watching.

Or were they?

Not far away, standing under another tree where a cat was clambering about in the branches, somebody – a boy with large spectacles – had seen everything.

CHAPTER THIRTEEN

FURTHER PANIC
THIS TIME
IN A SACK

BUMP! OOF! OUCH!

The sack landed heavily on the sand dunes, rolling and bumping until it came to a skidding stop.

Inside and bewildered, Mr Penguin and Colin lay on the ground blinking. Gordon settled himself down quite happily on Mr Penguin's belly and immediately fell asleep.

Mr Penguin shook his head to clear it. What HAD just happened? He ran through it all again. They'd gone to show the amulet and Edith's papers to Cynthia and Professor Umlaut, then someone had grabbed them and now here they were, where? In a bag in the desert.

He looked down at his empty flippers.

"The amulet and the papers!" gasped Mr Penguin. "GONE!"

There definitely had been bandits on the train then, and they'd been after Edith's special necklace. Well, they had it now.

Mr Penguin started to panic. He waddled about, stumbling and tripping as he tried to fight his way out of the sack.

Colin grabbed hold of his friend's ankle and Mr Penguin fell flat on his face.

CALM DOWN said Colin's pad, very firmly.

Colin stroked his chin for a moment, thoughtfully considering the pickle they were in. Then he ran, arm-legs flailing, at the tightly knotted end of the sack. For several minutes Colin tried to open it but he simply couldn't. Even his kung fu kicking legs were useless against it.

"Oh no…" wailed Mr Penguin, face down on the ground. "Now we are stuck out here in the desert – LOST! Probably miles from a town, miles from Edith and – "

He stopped abruptly and waggled his head about, listening.

He'd heard a noise. Something was outside the sack. He could hear it breathing.

He wailed again. "And now we are probably going to be gobbled up by… by…" He stopped, trying desperately to think of what in the desert might eat him. Lions? No. Tigers? No. Camels? Camels lived in the desert, he knew that. Did camels eat penguins?

He got up and started to do his panicky dance again. He hadn't got far when…

He crashed into something. The sack containing the Adventurers went flying, then whatever they had bumped into began pawing at the bag from outside.

Inside, Mr Penguin tried to run, but whatever was trying to get at them was holding them tight.

The knot at the top of the bag was being fumbled with.

Mr Penguin and Colin watched with widening eyes as the sack started to open.

They could see the dark sky.

Moonlight washed over them.

Mr Penguin's knees knocked.

Who was there?

He could hear breathing.

And then a face appeared.

It was the same face he'd seen at his window, looking at them with its one, glowing yellow eye.

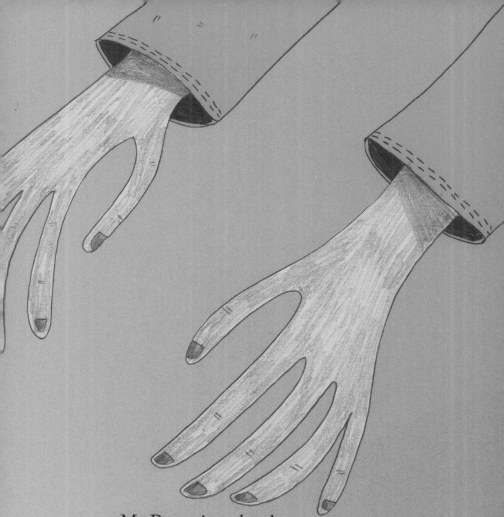

Mr Penguin yelped.

"Look!" he cried. "The face at the window!
And in the restaurant. A m-mummy!"

Then, before Mr Penguin or Colin
could do anything to stop it, two arms
reached into the sack and pulled them out.

CHAPTER FOURTEEN

EYEBALL

"AAAAAAAAAARGH!!!"
For the next five minutes Mr Penguin ran about with his eyes closed, yelling about cursed mummies, undead pharaohs and penguin-eating camels.

He only stopped when Colin
dived on him and held his pad in front
of his face.

It said:

STOP BEING A BANANAHEAD
YOU PLONKER AND

Next page:

LOOK!

Terrified, Mr Penguin looked and—

"Oh!" he exclaimed.

Instead of there being the bandage-
wrapped figure of a mummified pharaoh,
there was a boy with large spectacles. He
had a completely bald cat sitting on his
shoulder. The cat was wearing an eyepatch
and its one yellow eye was looking them
with interest.

Mr Penguin looked at the boy again
and the cogs in his brain whirred.

"I've seen you before," he said, trying
to remember. Think! Think! Think!

AHA!

"At the market!" cried Mr Penguin. "You helped me when that donkey threw me up into a date tree and my bum got stuck!"

The boy nodded, smiling, then introduced himself.

"My name is Farooq, and this is my cat. Her name is Iris but I call her Agent Eyeball because she is my number one assistant detective and main lookout and… well," he rubbed his nose, "well, also because she's only got one eyeball."

The cat meowed, proudly. Farooq started to

talk again, at high speed.

"I'm really glad we found you out here!" he said. "When we saw you thrown from the train we thought we'd lost you completely. But here you are! You aren't hurt, are you?"

Mr Penguin shook his head.

Farooq turned to face the railway line and shook his fist at the pinprick of light that was the Pyramid Express disappearing into the dark vastness of the desert.

"WHY THAT NO GOOD SCOUNDREL!" he yelled. "We knew there was going to be trouble, didn't we, Agent Eyeball? From the moment we saw that WANTED poster, we knew!"

Mr Penguin looked around. They were standing in the middle of the desert. All around them were sand dunes, but other than that – nothing. Mr Penguin was glad that he'd been rescued from the bag, but he really was very confused. What were a boy and his cat doing out here?

"How did you get here?" he asked.

Farooq grinned. "We followed you! We were on the train. We read in the newspaper that you were in town and then couldn't believe it when we met you in the market. We wanted to talk to you then, but there were too many people around."

He took a deep breath and told the Adventurers that his brother was a detective on the police force and that he always made fun of Farooq for wanting to be one too. He said that Farooq was too little and weedy and not clever enough to be a detective.

Colin rolled his eyes at this.

Farooq explained that he had decided to prove his brother wrong. Together, Farooq and Agent Eyeball were Mr Penguin's biggest fans and had read all about his adventures in the newspapers. They'd been inspired by him to start their own private detective agency called the Laghaz Secret Detective Club, of which they were both the co-directors and the only members.

At this, Farooq scrabbled about in his bag and pulled out his detective kit – a magnifying glass, a book about secret codes and a plump notebook. For weeks they had been training themselves to be detectives and every time they completed a new skill, Farooq had made himself a badge.

He stuck his chest out proudly so Mr Penguin could see a jangling array of homemade badges on his tunic.

"We are working on our Code-Breaking badge now," said Farooq. "After that I just need to get my "I've Eaten A Fish Finger Sandwich" badge and then I'll be a proper detective like you!"

Mr Penguin gulped. He didn't feel much like a proper detective at that very moment. He felt like a bit of an eejit. He was lost, his friend was lost, the amulet was lost, the clues Edith had hidden for them were lost and he had no idea what to do next. Farooq's mention of a fish finger sandwich briefly distracted him. He licked his beak, then, glancing down, he saw Colin glaring at him and holding up his pad

STOP THINKING ABOUT FOOD.

Mr Penguin cleared his throat and concentrated. "But why were you following us?" he asked. It can't have been to just show off their badges, nice though they were.

Farooq's face suddenly became serious.

"Because we've got something Very Important to tell you," he said. He looked around just in case anyone was disguised as a rock. They weren't, so he continued: "We thought it was you in the market, so we ran home to our office (my bedroom)

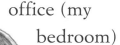

to get our notebook but when we got back, you'd gone. We came to your hotel later to catch you but that upset woman – Cynthia – was there. Then we followed you all to the library and overheard that your friend Edith had been kidnapped. Then we followed you to the train station and we couldn't believe what we saw. We were watching you from

the shadows waiting to board the train
and when we saw it, we knew we HAD to
get on. At first the train steward wouldn't
let us on to the platform, but we ducked
and dived and managed to slip past him
and jump on board just in time!"

Colin gave them a round of
applause. He was always impressed by
Daring Deeds.

"But what did you have to tell us?"
said Mr Penguin. Then, suddenly,
inspiration struck. "Do you know
something about Edith? Do you know
where she is?"

Farooq looked a bit puzzled. "I
don't think so," he said, then shook his
head. "No, but you were in great
danger on that train."

He dropped his voice
to a whisper. "There is a
master criminal on board!"

"Yes!" said Mr Penguin. "BANDITS! I knew there were. They must have been stowaways like you... I wonder who they are?"

Farooq beamed and stuck his chest out again with pride. "We know exactly who the master criminal is, don't we, Agent Eyeball?" he said, "And we saw everything!"

At this point Mr Penguin's eyes couldn't have grown any wider and he was beginning to quiver right from his shoelaces up to his hat.

"Who?" he whispered. In his mind came a vision of an enormous, fearsome bandit with a jutting, bristly jaw and a large bag thrown over his shoulder that said SWAG on it.

"Jasper Charade!" said Farooq.

"Who?" said Mr Penguin again.

He knew the name. He shook his

head to get the cogs whirring.

Prancing pyramids, that was it!
He'd seen it written down in Edith's
hidden papers.

"But there wasn't a Jasper
Charade," he said, his brow wrinkled.
"Colin borrowed a list of all the people in
our carriage and a Jasper Charade wasn't
on it."

"But he was!" said Farooq,
searching through his notebook until he
found what he was looking for. "I
managed to pinch this from the cabin
earlier. Look!"

He held up a passport. Mr Penguin
and Colin gasped.

They were looking at a photograph
of Mr Bland.

CHAPTER FIFTEEN

JASPER CHARADE

"Mr Bland?" said Mr Penguin, his beak flapping about in disbelief. "Nice, quiet, polite Mr Bland? With his neat napkin and piles of suitcases?"

Farooq nodded sternly.

"But how can Mr Bland be Jasper Charade?" said Mr Penguin. "Did he kidnap a real Mr Bland and take his place?"

"No," said Farooq, searching though his notebook again. "Mr Bland is a completely made-up person. Not only is Jasper Charade a master criminal, he is also a master of disguise."

Farooq pulled out a selection of newspaper clippings.

"Jasper Charade is also Hank Banjo, Cuthbert Verb AND Miss Precious Darling!"

Mr Penguin narrowed his eyes. "Are you sure?" He couldn't see how one person could so convincingly be all those different people.

But Colin could. He scuttled forward with his pen and drew long eyelashes and lipstick on the photo of Jasper Charade.

Mr Penguin gasped. He gasped so

ferociously he fell over.

It WAS true! Jasper Charade WAS all of these people.

And hang on! Hank Banjo? Cuthbert Verb? Miss Precious Darling? He'd seen these names before, again in Edith's papers. What did this all mean? Whilst he gathered his thoughts, Colin had his pad out again.

I THINK YOU NEED TO TELL US FROM THE BEGINNING

Farooq nodded.

He told them all about how, wanting to prove to his brother that he WAS clever enough to be a detective, he and Agent Eyeball cut mysterious stories out of the newspaper just in case they were Of Interest. They'd cut out all the same stories Edith had about the disappearances of Hank Banjo and Cuthbert Verb and Precious Darling... and they realised that wherever they had been, a theft had occurred too. At Hank Banjo's concerts, the singer had picked pockets as he walked through the audience, singing. Jasper had used the same trick as Miss Precious Darling. As Cuthbert Verb he'd pinched off people at book signings. Then, after each crime spree, he quite simply disappeared. Hank, Precious and Cuthbert had never been seen again.

It was only when Farooq had spotted this and had put the pictures from his collections together that he realised they were all the same person. He had wanted to tell Mr Penguin about it in the market so he could help them. And when he saw that person standing in front of Mr Penguin in the train queue, he couldn't believe it.

Sneaking on board, Farooq and Agent Eyeball had watched as Jasper Charade fiddled with the electrics before walking as calm as a cucumber into the dining car. When the lights went out, he'd run to the cabins and ransacked them. He searched through every case and trunk and hat box. He even messed up his own things to make it look like he had also been burgled by an Unknown Bandit.

"That must have been where that eyelash I thought was a ferocious insect

came from…" murmured Mr Penguin. It was part of Jasper's Precious Darling disguise.

Farooq continued, explaining how he'd sent Agent Eyeball to fetch Mr Penguin, but Mr Penguin had gone bonkers thinking that the cat was a cursed

mummy. (At this Agent Eyeball looked
VERY offended.)

Later, they had tiptoed into the
carriage to try again to tell Mr Penguin
and Colin about it all, and they had
seen Jasper Charade sneak up behind
them and throw them from the train.

"Then we leapt off to rescue you!"
said Farooq, and Agent Eyeball nodded.

Mr Penguin sat down heavily.

So it had been Jasper Charade
he'd heard earlier, talking about stealing
something. But who had he been
talking to?

"What I don't understand is why
Mr Bland – I mean, Jasper Charade
– was on the Pyramid Express? Do you
think he just decided to ransack all the
carriages to see what he could find?"

Colin shook his head and
scribbled on his pad.

NO it said BECAUSE IF SO HE WOULD HAVE NICKED ANYTHING VALUABLE

BUT HE

Next page:

DIDN'T.

Farooq pushed his specs up his nose. "So he was definitely after that amulet," he said. "It seems like he knew it was, or at least thought it MIGHT be, on the train." Agent Eyeball nodded again.

For a moment everyone was silent. Everyone except Gordon, who was snoring as loudly as a fully grown hog. In the semi silence, everyone was thinking big thoughts.

It was Colin who spoke first.

I THINK EDITH HAD DISCOVERED ALL OF THIS said Colin's pad, and they all agreed. It did seem like Edith had been on the trail.

Had Jasper arranged to have Edith kidnapped by someone? What did he want the amulet for?

Mr Penguin gulped at the thought. He didn't know any of the answers, but he did know two things:

1. That everything felt like it was leading in a very dangerous direction and
2. Whatever WAS going on, Edith seemed to be the key to it all.

Edith was still missing, and now Cynthia and Professor Umlaut were stuck on a train with a master criminal.

"We have to get to Cynthia and Professor Umlaut, and find Edith," Mr Penguin said. His flippers quivered, because what he really wanted to do was lie down and only get up when everything was back to being jolly. He said in a thin little voice: "We need to get to the Valley of Peril as soon as possible. But how?"

He looked around. There was just vast emptiness all around them.

"Easy!" said Farooq, smiling. "They'll take us," he added, pointing.

Mr Penguin squinted. Not far away there were some shapes that he had mistaken for piles of sand and rocks. One of the shapes yawned and he realised that he had been mistaken.

"Oh no!" he cried, "not DONKEYS again!"

NO said Colin's pad. He turned the page.

It said one word:

CAMELS.

CHAPTER SIXTEEN

THE VALLEY OF PERIL

The night-time dash on camelback through the desert did not go well for Mr Penguin.

In front of him, Farooq, Agent Eyeball, Colin and even Gordon managed to sit sensibly on the backs of the beasts as they hoofed it through the darkness. Mr Penguin didn't. He was thrown about

all over the place, unable
to stay upright for a second. He spent
much of the journey dangling upside
down from his umbrella, holding on to
his hat. Even a line of web from Colin's
bottom didn't hold him on properly.

Why is everyone else so good at
everything? he wondered as he boinged
about. And why aren't I good at
ANYTHING?

Eventually, Mr Penguin found
some sticky dates in his satchel and,
sticking two of them to his bum, he
managed to glue himself to the camel's
back. It wasn't comfortable, but it was a
Solution Of Sorts.

On they trekked through the desert. Mr Penguin was surprised to find that once the burning heat of the day had vanished with the sun, the desert was as cold and shivery as the time he had got himself stuck inside a refrigerator. Before long a pale glimmer of sunlight peeked above the horizon. As dawn broke, the five Adventurers found themselves standing on the top of a sand dune looking down on the Valley of Peril. The desert was already beginning to heat up yet, strangely, this place felt chilly, like a haunted attic.

Everything was sinister and silent. All Mr Penguin could hear was his heart hammering in his chest. Even Gordon seemed to find it spooky and dived under Mr Penguin's hat for safety.

The Adventurers hopped off their camels and surveyed the scene. There were enormous pyramids and huge bits of ruined buildings jutting out from the sand. In the pale, early light they looked like ghostly hands reaching out to grab you, and through it all an otherworldly mist snaked and slithered about.

"Perhaps," whispered Mr Penguin, "we could just find somewhere far away from here where we could just have a nice, safe sit-down?"

His stomach rumbled. There was the leftover half of the fish finger sandwich he'd scraped up from the floor of his train carriage that he wanted to swallow whole. (He didn't mind that it had bits of carpet fluff on it.) But he knew he couldn't tuck in to it right now. They had Edith to find and Cynthia and Professor Umlaut to rescue – besides which, Colin was now scampering down into the valley humming his action music again. He was investigating something.

Mr Penguin, Farooq and Agent Eyeball hurried after him. The strange mist curled icily around them, making them shiver. They lost sight of Colin, but found him again when he shouted for them. He did this by scribbling LOOK AT THIS on his pad and hurling it at Mr Penguin, hitting him on the head with a bump.

Colin was staring at the ground. Farooq and Mr Penguin pulled out their magnifying glasses and studied the footprints in the sand, stretching out into the mist.

"Edith's kidnapper?" said Farooq. "We must follow them!"

"Must we?" trembled Mr Penguin, but he shuffled

through the sand after his friends.

The footsteps twisted and turned through the crumbling ruins, and as he waddled Mr Penguin's thoughts turned to the book he and Colin had been reading. The eerie mist, the abandoned temples and tombs, the pyramids – they had all been in the book and pointed to one thing: mummies.

Mr Penguin gulped. This strange place must be littered with ancient mummies just waiting to leap out and give him the screaming abdabs.

He was so lost in thought that he didn't realise until he bumped into them that the rest of the gang had halted. A chill wind cleared the mist so they could see what was in front of them. In the shadow of an enormous pyramid a short distance away was a giant mound of sand,

and at the base of that was the most extraordinary entrance to a building Mr Penguin had ever seen. Vast and ornate, it seemed as if the desert had whipped it up magically by itself.

The footprints led up to the open doorway and so, trembling, Mr Penguin followed Colin, Farooq and Agent Eyeball. They slipped into the darkness and down a long, sand-dusted staircase. The stone walls were carved with hieroglyphics and lit with an orangey glow. The light was coming from a room beyond.

The Adventurers continued their descent until they arrived in a chamber. Torches burned and flickered, making it seem like the carved walls were moving all by themselves. Circling the room were huge carved statues of people – but instead of human heads, one had the head of a hawk, another the head of a jackal, the next an alligator.

Mr Penguin was so terrified he had to clamp his flippers over his beak to stop it chattering. This was DEFINITELY the place a cursed mummy would leap out and grab him.

And no sooner had that thought crossed his mind when a hand reached out of the darkness and tapped him on the shoulder.

CHAPTER SEVENTEEN

WHO SHOULD WE BE WORRIED ABOUT?

Mr Penguin jumped so high that had he been outside someone would have had to have scraped him off the moon with a fish slice.

He spun around and hardly dared
to look at what dreadful, bandage-
wrapped monster had tapped him, but,
OH!

It was Edith!

"Hello boys!" she said.

Colin and Mr Penguin hugged her
tightly and quickly introduced Farooq and
Agent Eyeball. At the sound of Edith's
voice, Gordon leapt out from under Mr
Penguin's hat and honked like a foghorn
before nesting down happily on her head.

"We've been so worried about you!"
cried Mr Penguin. He was delighted, but
Edith looked serious.

"Have you brought the police with
you?" she said.

"No?" said Mr Penguin. Then, thinking fast, he said: "But if your kidnappers are around, Colin can do some kung fu on them and Farooq can wallop them with his bag and I... well, I can just shout lots of Encouraging Things and—"

Edith interrupted him.

"Kidnappers?" she said. "What kidnappers?"

Mr Penguin was perplexed. "The people who snatched you away from the library and brought you here!" he explained, but Edith shook her head.

"No, no!" she said. "That's not what happened at all. I had to come here to warn – well, I'll tell you all about that in a minute. I left a note with Gordon to give to you, telling you to follow me and bring the police. I wonder what happened to it?"

WE FOUND THE TRAIN TIMETABLE said Colin's pad.

"But no note," said Mr Penguin.

Before anyone could say anything else, they were distracted by Gordon. He'd stood up on Edith's head and had his beak clamped around the arm of one of the statues, trying to eat it whole. Everyone knew what had happened to Edith's message: Gordon had eaten it.

"Never mind," said Edith, tickling Gordon under his chin. "You're here now and hopefully everything will be OK. I just need to find—"

But it was Mr Penguin's turn to interrupt this time.

"OH NO!" he cried. "But we aren't safe, are we Farooq?" And Farooq explained everything that had happened. He told Edith about Hank Banjo, Cuthbert Verb and Miss Precious Darling all being Mr Bland... except Mr Bland was actually called Jasper Charade.

"But you knew all of that, didn't you?" said Mr Penguin, and Edith nodded.

"I've been on HIS case for months," she said.

"Jasper threw Mr Penguin and Colin and Gordon OUT OF THE TRAIN!" cried Farooq, his specs sliding down his nose.

Then Mr Penguin told her about Jasper ransacking the train. "He's a very dangerous thief, isn't he?" he said.

Edith nodded again. On her head, Gordon stopped trying to eat the statue and listened. He'd heard something. There were faint noises coming from outside.

SOMEONE'S COMING said Colin's pad.

Footsteps started to descend the stairs.

"Oh!" said Mr Penguin, cheerfully. "It might be the police! We're saved!"

He went to waddle to the stairs, but Edith pulled him back and they ran to hide in a dark corner of the chamber.

Mr Penguin's eyes were wide. "That's probably an ancient mummy coming to get us," he whispered.

DON'T BE A BANANA, MR PENGUIN said Colin's pad.

They all listened again and now there was the murmur of a voice.

"Is that Jasper Charade?" whispered Farooq, straining his ears to listen.

The Adventurers held their breaths as the shadow of a figure was projected into the room.

Edith shook her head. "No, Jasper is certainly a dreadful crook," she whispered. "But he isn't the one we should be worried about..."

"Who SHOULD we be worried about?" said Mr Penguin, conscious of how loudly his knees were now knocking.

Edith's eyes followed the figure as it stepped into the chamber.

"Cynthia," she hissed.

CHAPTER EIGHTEEN

LAUGHING LIKE A
CRAZED HYENA

"Cynthia?" gasped Mr Penguin and
Farooq at the same time. They
were both immediately poked by Colin
and Agent Eyeball, telling them to keep
their voices down.

Edith nodded. "She's always been trouble," she said.

Farooq looked as if was thinking very seriously about something. He shoved his specs up his nose again.

"Of course!" he said. "Agent Eyeball and I saw Cynthia yesterday in the market. She was waiting around in the shadows for someone and then when you walked into the library, Edith, she followed you. I wrote it all down in my detective notebook."

Edith nodded, seemingly unsurprised by this news. Mr Penguin WAS surprised though. His beak was hanging open.

"Yes," Edith muttered. "She followed me in all right. Got me into a tight corner. I wanted to talk to her but, well, she had other ideas. That's when I realised I had to scarper. Gordon caused a distraction, I stashed my special book with my papers hidden in it and hopped out of the window. Gordon had that note telling you to get the police and follow me here. He was meant to show you where my notes were in their hiding place…"

"Oh, he did!" said Mr Penguin. "Eventually."

"I knew Cynthia would follow me, but I needed a head-start to tell—"

Edith cut herself off as just then Cynthia was followed into the room by three other figures. Mr Penguin, peeping from behind the column, recognised them immediately – Professor Umlaut, Mr Bland-who-was-actually-called-Jasper-Charade and Dr Fossil.

If Cynthia was dangerous, shouldn't they be trying to rescue or at least warn Professor Umlaut? thought Mr Penguin. He whispered to Edith, but she shook her head.

"No," she said. "He's in on it too – he's Cynthia's husband."

Mr Penguin was flabbergasted. Every time he thought he understood something, the more he realised he didn't understand anything at all. In on WHAT? he wondered. He was just about to whisper a flood of questions when Colin walloped him on the bottom with his pad.

LISTEN it said.

So, holding their breaths, the Adventurers earwigged.

"You good-for-nothing thief, Cynthia!" Jasper Charade snarled. All the politeness of his Mr Bland character had vanished. "Give me back my amulet!"

"YEAH!" cried Dr Fossil. "And give me back MINE n'all!"

But Cynthia just laughed. It wasn't jolly HA-HA-BONK sort of laugh, but a laugh like a crazed hyena.

"You must think I'm stupid," grumbled Dr Fossil. "I knew there was something fishy about that driver who delivered my museum's new sarcophagus. It was dark, but I still recognised you, Umlaut."

Professor Umlaut jumped, looking more like a startled rabbit than ever.

"Disguises are my thing, so I saw through yours too," said Jasper Charade to the professor. "Coming to the stage door dressed as a girl scout wanting to sell me cookies – it was one in the morning! And I've never seen a girl scout with a moustache! And all the time you, Cynthia, were in my dressing room stealing MY amulet. Give it back or… or… we'll call the police!"

Cynthia laughed again and then said, "Shut your pie holes, the pair of you! Call the police, indeed! I don't think so. You, Jasper, a wanted jewel thief and you, Bernard, with all those stolen items in your museum. Getting the police involved would be the last thing either of you would do. Yes, I stole your amulets – and I've got Edith's too after that idiot penguin simply handed it to me. I must say that was good work throwing him off the train, Jasper."

Behind the statue, Mr Penguin suddenly realised the voice that he'd heard talking about stealing jigsaws had been Cynthia. She'd been talking to Professor Umlaut.

Mr Penguin quickly ran through

everything he now knew – Cynthia was behind whatever had been going on and had stolen amulets from both Jasper Charade and Dr Fossil, both of whom were also robbers! And she had tried to steal an amulet from Edith too. All of this had been going on right under his beak and he hadn't seen any of it. He suddenly felt a bit hot about the bow tie, thinking how he had given Edith's necklace to Cynthia. How silly!

Jasper, angry as he was, nodded. "Well, I thought those twerps were involved," he mumbled.

"Those idiots ate up every fib we told them," laughed Cynthia. "And it worked! Here we are, right where I need to be, with these!"

From her handbag she pulled four identical golden amulets. Where she'd got the fourth one, Mr Penguin didn't know.

The amulets glinted in the torchlight
as Cynthia started to scan the walls of the
chamber, grinning wildly. The Adventurers
withdrew further into the shadows.

"What are you looking for?" cried

Dr Fossil. "What IS this all about? What do you need all these amulets for? You have your own!"

Ah! thought Mr Penguin, that's where the fourth one had come from. Cynthia had her own one all the time. Mr Penguin scratched his head. He'd never seen an amulet until a few hours ago and now everyone seemed to have one. Nice as they were, Mr Penguin really would have preferred a trayful of fish finger sandwiches. Trembling, he tuned back into what the crooks were saying. And boy! Was he glad he did. Because Jasper suddenly said something which surprised all the Adventurers hiding behind the statue.

"Yeah!" cried Jasper. His face was pink with anger again. "What do you need them all for? Mother gave one to each of us!"

Mother?

Mr Penguin, Colin, Farooq and Agent Eyeball all swivelled to look at Edith. She nodded.

"Yes," she whispered. "Jasper and Bernard are my brothers."

CHAPTER NINETEEN

LIKE A JIGSAW

T he siblings in the chamber started
squabbling and the noise covered
Edith whispering an explanation.

She sighed. "We're all brothers and sisters. Bernard's the oldest and Jasper's the baby."

The photo in Edith's papers popped into Mr Penguin's mind. Edith and Cynthia as girls with their mum and dad. The other children weren't friends, like he'd assumed, but her brothers.

"Mother used to take us on their archaeology trips, and we all used to get on very well. But I think being surrounded by lots of exciting and precious treasures went to my brothers' heads. I've discovered that Bernard's museum is FULL of things he's pilfered from around the world. And Jasper has always loved dressing up and sparkly things. He's a very talented pickpocket. I didn't think Cynthia was a crook until recently, though, when I started investigating the stolen amulets."

Suddenly, Cynthia's voice rang out loudly in the chamber.

"ENOUGH!" she yelled, and her brothers stopped squabbling immediately.

Cynthia sighed. "All right, I'll tell you. Mother gave us these amulets as presents all those years ago – she'd found them on some of her digs, but she didn't know what they really were. They are pieces of a giant, ancient key. A key that opens a tomb hidden behind one of these walls. I discovered all of this when I was researching my latest book, didn't I, Umlaut?"

Umlaut squeaked nervously.

"You mean, behind these walls is an unopened tomb?" gasped Dr Fossil, excitedly.

"Full of treasures?" cried Jasper, his eyes gleaming.

"YOU BETCHA!" said Cynthia,

smugly. "And something else, even more important!"

Mr Penguin gulped. There was a lot he wasn't raving about with regards to his current situation, but now with this talk of opening tombs, he could hardly keep himself from yelping with terror. There was an army of ancient mummies behind that wall, he was sure. Colin patted him soothingly on the shoe, but it didn't help much.

Cynthia cried out in delight, making Mr Penguin jump.

"AHA!" she said, and Mr Penguin saw that she was running her hand along the wall opposite his hiding place. She pressed something and a circular section of the wall slid inwards.

Then, transfixed, everyone in the chamber watched as Cynthia set about clicking the four amulets together so that they made a large, golden disc.

IT'S LIKE A JIGSAW said Colin's pad.

She clicked the disc into place. It sat like a large golden ball of poop on top of a picture of a dung beetle carved on to the wall.

At this point, Mr Penguin was so concerned about a cursed mummy appearing that he could hardly concentrate on anything, but he realised that beside him, Edith was chuckling.

"It'll never work!" she chortled. From her bumbag she took out a FIFTH amulet.

"ANOTHER ONE?" goggled Mr Penguin. Everyone shushed him.

Edith nodded.

"The one in your sandwich was a fake! I had it made just in case. It'll never open the tomb!" she whispered. "Quick, whilst they are distracted we can scarper out and—"

"Get the police?' said Farooq.

Edith nodded and, as silently as they could, the Adventurers began tiptoeing to the staircase.

At the opposite wall, it was dawning on the crooks that something wasn't right.

"It's not working!" snarled Jasper.

Cynthia, for the first time, looked a bit ruffled. She kept examining the golden disc and prodding it angrily.

The Adventurers continued their tiptoeing. Mr Penguin couldn't keep his eyes from the wall, thinking that any moment a mummy would burst out, trembling from his hat to his sand-covered shoes. There was only thing that would help him. He slipped his flipper into his satchel and pulled out his lunchbox. He was just about to open it when he misjudged his step.

The lunchbox went flying.

In slow motion it flew through the air before landing with a CRASH on the ancient stone floor.

Mr Penguin gulped as Cynthia, Professor Umlaut, Dr Fossil and Jasper Charade all spun around on the spot, their eyes glued directly on him.

CHAPTER TWENTY

A WIDE VARIETY OF BOOBYTRAPS

It didn't take long for the Adventurers to find themselves captured by the crooks.

They put up a good fight – Edith swirled her bumbag over her head and walloped Dr Fossil, Colin biffed Jasper on the nose, Farooq and Agent Eyeball clonked Professor Umlaut all over with the book from their bag. Mr Penguin stood in the middle of it with his lunchbox, knees knocking, yelling, "OH MY HADDOCK GOUJONS!" in dismay. But before long Jasper, who was strong as well as tall, had captured them all.

Cynthia had then discovered Edith's switch-a-roo with the pretend amulet.

Seething, she grabbed the real one, jammed it into the jigsaw and pushed it into the wall.

Dangerously loud whirring sounded deep beneath the chamber.

Cynthia began turning the disc like a key, and Edith cried out: "No – not that way or you'll—"

"Don't tell me what to do!"
snapped Cynthia, and she yanked the disc
sharply to the left.

Suddenly a vast section of the
chamber floor crumbled away, revealing
a deep, dark hole. Mr Penguin
wobbled at the edge of it but was
caught by Colin at the last moment.

"Cynthia!" said Edith.
"You really must listen
to me! This place is full

of a wide variety of booby traps. That's a bottomless pit!"

Mr Penguin gasped. One misstep and he'd have disappeared into the centre of the earth!

Cynthia laughed again. "You're always trying to ruin my fun!" she said. "But not this time. This time Little Cynthia has made the discovery of a lifetime and it'll be ALL MINE! Not Boring Bernard's! Not Jazzy Jasper's and not Goody Two Shoes Edith's!"

"What are you talking about?" snapped Dr Fossil.

"Yes!" piped up Mr Penguin. "I would also like to know what is happening."

Cynthia seized this moment and with all eyes on her, began her story.

"You have always thought you were better than me, but it was ME who found this place. Sure, there will be interesting finds behind this wall, but I've discovered something priceless!"

She cleared her throat. "Many thousands of years ago," she began, in a voice like she was reading from a story book, "a pharaoh was given the gift of a ring from the Sun God. The stone set into it was the Sun Stone – a gem made from a single drop of the sun's fire. This ring wasn't just beautiful – it was magical too. Whoever wears the ring can turn anything they touch to solid gold!"

"No, Cynthia, you REALLY need to listen to me!" said Edith. "You've haven't got that—"

But Cynthia didn't listen.

"No!" she shouted. "It's going to be mine and mine alone!"

And with a sharp jerk she twisted
the golden disc in the wall again, this time
to the right.

There were more deep mechanical
grumblings and the entire wall of the
chamber split apart.

Mr Penguin squeezed his eyes shut
and held his breath, waiting for an ancient
mummy to spring out. When that didn't
happen, he risked a peek.

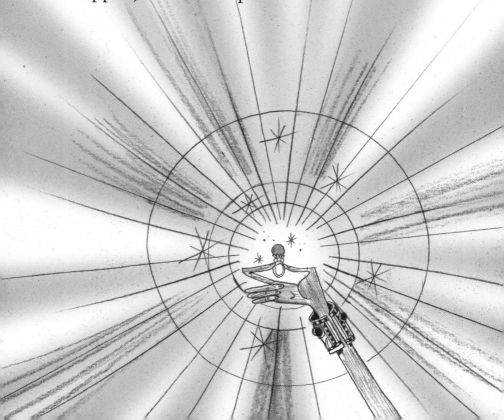

No mummies, but instead another gigantic wall. It was solid, gleaming gold. There were some hieroglyphics carved on to it.

"What does it say?" hissed Mr Penguin.

Edith was a whizz at lots of things, from engineering to flying plans. She could also read hieroglyphics, so she quickly translated it.

"It says: 'HAHAHA YOU DIDN'T THINK IT WOULD BE THAT EASY DID YOU?' but that has been crossed out and then it says: 'CALAMITY SHALL COME ON SWIFT WINGS TO ANYONE WHO DISTURBS THIS TOMB.' See – I told you," continued Edith. "This whole place is boobytrapped. It's VERY dangerous!"

Calamity! Danger! Mr Penguin's knees knocked again.

But Cynthia continued to ignore Edith. Grinning, she found a small door hidden in the golden wall and pushed it open.

A gust of hot, dry air whistled through, making Mr Penguin's beak twitch and a shiver run down his back. The dust settled and everyone could see that it was the entrance to a tunnel.

"That Sun Stone ring will be mine!" cried Cynthia, and she went to duck through the doorway.

WHOOSH! A razor-sharp golden sword swung – SNIP! SNAP! – across the entrance. Cynthia leapt back just in time, but it sliced a large hole in the knee of her slacks.

BOOBYTRAPPED said Colin's pad helpfully.

Cynthia thought for a moment.

"Yes," she purred. "Perhaps you are

right, sister dear. This place IS rather dangerous. Too dangerous for me."

Her eyes locked on to Mr Penguin.

"You'll have to find it for me," she said. "You are just the right size for that tunnel."

Mr Penguin felt as if his bow tie had suddenly tightened.

"Um, I'd rather not if that is OK

with you?" he said quietly, then he gave
Cynthia his nice smile.

But in a flash Cynthia had reached
into the tunnel, swiped the sword and was
waggling it in Mr Penguin's direction,
making him shuffle dangerously close to
the bottomless pit and towards the tunnel
door. Edith and Farooq shouted out in
horror and Agent Eyeball yowled loudly.
Colin leapt to Mr Penguin's side and
danced about with his fists up.

"Really, Cynthia," pleaded Professor
Umlaut, but she just told him to quit
yipping.

"Wait!" said Dr Fossil. "How do you
know that penguin isn't going to keep the
ring for himself?'

The three crooks in the room all
narrowed their eyes at Mr Penguin.

"Good point!" said Cynthia,
considering the problem. Then she had an
idea. "I'll need some insurance!" And
before Mr Penguin knew what was
happening she'd got her brothers to dangle
Edith and Gordon over the bottomless pit.

Cynthia checked her wristwatch.

"You have thirty minutes to find me
the ring," she said. "If you don't, your
friends will be going for a little trip. SO
NO FUNNY BUSINESS!"

Mr Penguin peered over the side of
the pit. It was so dark that it made his eyes
fizz and tingle. He had no choice – he'd
have to go into the boobytrapped tunnel
and find the ring, or else Edith and
Gordon would… He gulped. It didn't bear
thinking about.

I AM COMING WITH YOU said

Colin's pad.

Then Farooq stamped hard on Professor Umlaut's foot. The shock made the professor release him and Agent Eyeball and they raced to Mr Penguin's side.

"We're coming too!" said Farooq and he shoved his glasses up his nose, decisively.

"You'll need this!" croaked Edith. Her voice sounded a bit funny because she was upside down. She rummaged in her bumbag, pulled out her notebook and hurled it at Mr Penguin. He missed it, of course, but Colin grabbed it. "It'll help! Use your brain, Mr Penguin!" said Edith.

Cynthia waggled the sword menacingly again – and because there was nothing else they could do, the Adventurers ducked under the doorway and into the ancient tomb.

CHAPTER TWENTY-ONE

BANDAGES

The second Mr Penguin set foot inside the dimly lit tunnel, the floor buckled under his feet, and turned into a giant slide.

WHOOSH!

Down the Adventurers slid, dust and
cobwebs flying in their faces... and every
few seconds – SNIP! SNAP! – more razor-
sharp swords flashed in front of their faces.

Colin, excellent in any perilous
situation, hurdled over his friends and –
KAPOW! – kung fu kicked the swords out
of the way.

Eventually, and with an enormous
THUD!, the four intrepid investigators
landed heavily in another room.

And oh boy was it dark! Thick, heavy
blackness surrounded the Adventurers and
Mr Penguin's imagination started to run
riot. He just knew mummies were waiting
in the darkness to spook him.

"Hang on!" whispered Farooq,
beside him. He rummaged in his bag and
with a click the room lit up with the light
from a tiny torch.

"From my detective kit!" grinned

Farooq. Mr Penguin sighed. He'd packed his sandwiches instead of a sensible torch.

There were, thankfully, no mummies to be seen, but there were lots of other things. The torch only cast a small ring of light, so shuffling about as a group, they investigated the space. It was packed with objects: statues, chests, giant jars, even a chariot.

"This is a burial chamber," said Farooq, looking about with wonder. "Pharaohs were buried with the things they'd need in the afterlife. Strange that there isn't a sarcophagus though… Oh wait! Yes there is!"

Farooq held the torch up and Mr Penguin yelped, for there, in the middle of the chamber, was a stone coffin. And what made the creepy scene worse was that the lid was slightly open!

Mr Penguin's feet were knocking

about like billy-o. He started to do his funny panicky dance, but found that Colin had already wrapped a length of bum-web around his legs so he couldn't dash about doing himself a mischief.

Agent Eyeball sniffed the sarcophagus suspiciously, then Farooq bravely leant over and peered inside.

"Oh!" he exclaimed. "It's just full of old bandages!" And he held up a handful of the grubby fabric.

Well, this was too much for Mr Penguin. An empty sarcophagus and a pile of old bandages could only mean one thing ...

"A NAKED ZOMBIE PHARAOH IS GOING TO LEAP OUT AT ANY MOMENT!" he cried, and, snapping himself free from Colin's lasso, begin charging about the chamber with his flippers waggling and his bottom wobbling from side to side.

Crash! BANG! WALLOP! Objects went flying.

CALM DOWN, MR PENGUIN! said Colin's pad, but Mr Penguin couldn't.

He bumped into a model boat, sending it flying, and staggered backwards into the far wall. A stone behind him shifted and there was a strange clunking noise from above them. A fine shower of dust and sand rained down.

UH OH! said Colin's pad.

And on the next page he drew an arrow.

They all looked up.

Above them, row upon row of dangerously sharp spikes had appeared from the ceiling. A whirring noise started and the Adventurers watched with wild, wide eyes as the spiked ceiling slowly crept towards them.

"Quick!" cried Farooq. "To the tunnel!"

And it was then that they realised the tunnel they had tumbled through only a few minutes before had disappeared! It was as if the wall had grown over it and hidden it from sight.

It meant one thing: they were trapped!

CHAPTER TWENTY-TWO

MOTHER KNOWS BEST

The walls of the chamber were large, rough stone slabs and nowhere was there a door. Meanwhile, the spiked ceiling continued to creep closer.

"We'll be squashed as flat as pancakes!" hissed Farooq.

"Ooh!" said Mr Penguin, and his tummy grumbled as a vision of fluffy pancakes danced in his head. Colin clonked him on the ankle with his pen and the image vanished. He had to concentrate.

"There MUST be a way out!" said Farooq. "But where?"

Agent Eyeball suddenly meowed and pointed her tail at Mr Penguin.

GOOD IDEA said Colin's pad.

EDITH MIGHT BE ABLE TO HELP US!

Edith? thought Mr Penguin. But she's upstairs being dangled over a pit! Then he realised Agent Eyeball was pointing at Edith's notebook.

The gang gathered around and flicked through it, Farooq holding the candle so they could see.

The book was filled with all sorts

of things: a knitting pattern for a new swimming costume for Gordon, recipes, shopping lists. One page just said BUY TURNIPS. But eventually they found something that looked promising.

It was a page that looked like a wax rubbing of an ancient tablet, covered in a complicated language. On the other side were scribbled notes where Edith had translated the ancient text.

It said: THE SUN GOD'S TOMB OF DOOM.

Mr Penguin shook as Colin read out loud on his pad, carefully copying bits out and holding them up for everyone else to read.

TO FIND THE RING...

THREE TASKS IN THE TOMB ETC. ETC.

FIRST TASK: "MOTHER KNOWS BEST"

CRACK THE CODE TO FIND THE DOOR.

The Adventurers all looked at each other. They'd searched for the door but without success, and now they had to crack a code? Mr Penguin found that all he could think about were the spikes getting closer and closer. Already he could see himself reflected in them. Another few minutes and they'd be spiked and flattened.

"Mother?" said Farooq, then snapped his fingers. "Of course – another word for mother is mummy! The code must be something to do with the sarcophagus."

"But there's nothing but those smelly old bandages in it!" quivered Mr Penguin.

Farooq picked the bandages up again and Mr Penguin held a squeak in

with his flipper – he was still worried
about naked zombie pharaohs.

Suddenly there was a loud CRUNCH!

The ceiling had dropped low enough
to start squashing some of the objects in
the room. The head fell off a giant statue
near a large jar and tumbled to the floor.
Mr Penguin's knees knocked and he ran
around the sarcophagus in a circle until
Colin's pad walloped him on the head.

STOP IT it said.

LOOK HERE!

Mr Penguin did as he was told, joining Farooq peering at the bandages through his magnifying glass.

"They're covered in writing!" said Mr Penguin. The bandages were actually one long continuous strip of fabric and inked with hieroglyphics.

"What does it say?" said Mr Penguin, but nobody knew.

IT IS A CODE said Colin.

Mr Penguin wished Edith were there. She was clever at codebreaking. Not for the first time, Mr Penguin felt a bit useless. All he'd done was release the spikes.

The ceiling crunched down again, crumbling another of the statues. The spikes were creeping closer towards the Adventurers' heads.

"Quick!" squeaked Mr Penguin.

Farooq was now full of action. Into his bag he went and he pulled out the book from the library.

Codebreaking for Beginners by Anita Clue.

"This should help!" he grinned, flicking through the pages. "Morse code? No... Shift Cipher? No... AHA!"

He showed them a page. "Scytale Cipher."

Farooq, reading at the speed of light, explained that this type of code involves lots of letters written on a long piece of paper – OR BANDAGE, said Colin – and it only makes sense when the paper – OR BANDAGE, said Colin – was wrapped around something and the correct letters lined up properly.

CRUNCH! The ceiling collapsed further, crushing the largest jar to pieces. Dust billowed around the room and

Agent Eyeball yowled.

"We need something to wrap it around!" said Farooq. "Something mummy-sized…"

Mr Penguin felt Farooq's eyes on him, sizing him up.

"Mr Penguin, you're the same size as this sarcophagus. Quick! Wrap yourself up!"

Mr Penguin was horrified. Wind those stinky old bandages around himself? Not for a million fish finger sandwiches!

More awful crunching sounds echoed around the chamber.

A voice boomed from far away. It was Cynthia.

"MR PENGUIN?" she cried in a horrible voice. "MY BROTHERS' HANDS ARE GETTING SLIPPY!"

Mr Penguin gasped. Edith and

Gordon! They needed him.
He squeezed his eyes
shut as Colin wound the bandages
around him until he looked like a
mummy. Farooq, Colin and Agent
Eyeball peered at him. The hieroglyphics
were all stretched out over his belly, and
together, Colin and Farooq translated

them with Edith's notebook.
Mr Penguin tried not to
look at the roof which was just
inches above them.

Farooq peered doubtfully
at the book. "Edith seems to have
found this riddle in her researches
already," he said. "She's come up with
her own version of it here…"

WHEN IS A DOOR NOT A
DOOR? Colin read from the notebook.

"What on earth does THAT mean?"
said Mr Penguin. A door is always a
door! Except when there wasn't one to
escape through from a crunching, spiking,
squishing ceiling! If Edith already knew
the answer to the riddle, why couldn't she
just have written it down?

Colin clicked one of his foot-hands.

I KNOW THE ANSWER! said his
pad.

IT'S A JAR

Huh? Mr Penguin pointed to the side of the room where the giant jars were.

"They are over there!" he said, wondering what on earth his friend could want from a jar, especially Colin who was always telling HIM off for thinking about food.

The pad was out again:

NO YOU PLONKER!

And Colin hauled Mr Penguin towards the jars.

Farooq and Agent Eyeball followed. They had to crouch as the ceiling was getting so low now. "When a door is open a bit," said Farooq, "you can say it's ajar!"

"Oh!" said Mr Penguin, remembering. "Like on the train!"

He raced after his friends. The roof was making such awful sounds and

the sharp spikes gleamed in the fading
torchlight.

Colin was examining the jars closely.
Then he found it! A tiny carving on one of
the jars – a picture of the amulets Cynthia
had stolen.

Colin kicked it with a kung fu kick
and a tiny concealed door sprang open in
the wall.

"Quickly!" said Farooq.

Colin and Agent Eyeball sprang in
like acrobats, followed by Farooq. Now it

was Mr Penguin's turn, but the bandages he was wearing caught on a jutting piece of broken statue. He spun like a spinning top around the room.

The ceiling was still thundering down.

Colin fired out a bum-web lasso, caught Mr Penguin by the ankle and heaved him across the floor. The spikes were almost on him. Mr Penguin squeezed his eyes shut and then…

CRUNCH.

The ceiling crashed on to the floor.

CHAPTER TWENTY-THREE

THE FLOOR
IS LAVA

Mr Penguin, with his eyes closed, patted himself down to see if he was now a pancake.

He wasn't.

His nice plump belly was still there and he was also, he realised, still alive.

"That was close!" panted Farooq, shaking his torch to get the batteries to work a little longer. "What now?"

Mr Penguin started to reach into his bag for his lunchbox. He needed a bite of his sandwich to Sustain him, but Colin gave him A Look. It meant: NOT NOW, MR PENGUIN! WE HAVE A RING TO FIND AND FRIENDS TO RESCUE. Mr Penguin smiled sheepishly and pretended he had just been checking his bag was OK.

This new tunnel they found themselves in was dark and so small they had to crawl through it. Mr Penguin had to hum to himself to block out the sounds he could hear through the walls. There were things crawling about, he just knew it, and he was sure he could hear something bubbling. A mummy? No – zombies don't tend to do much messing about with bubbles.

It was also stiflingly hot. Eventually there was a light at the end of the tunnel, and they shuffled at speed towards it. Mr Penguin burst out of it with glee then – YIKES! – found himself beginning to fall through thin air!

His friends pulled him to safety. They gazed around the enormous new room and discovered they were teetering on the very edge of a thin stone platform. Stretching out in front of them was a vast amount of empty space broken only by a strange collection of tall pillars, their bases disappearing into the gloom below.

Mr Penguin was terrifically confused. What was this place? Then Farooq tapped him on the shoulder and pointed. On the far side of the room were two doors set into the wall. One was golden and the other plain, dusty stone.

The four pals realised that

somehow or other they had to cross this space. They couldn't go back – the previous room had been flattened by the spiked ceiling. But how could they cross the room?

Colin surveyed the scene under his monobrow.

THESE PILLARS ARE STEPPING STONES said his pad.

Mr Penguin breathed a sigh of relief. He'd wondered if they were going to have to build some sort of bridge, but he only had a brolly, some books and a lunchbox in his bag. Stepping stones, albeit very high dangerous ones, were an easier option.

Mr Penguin peered at them and noticed that some of the pillars were golden and the others were stone. "AHA!" he said, pleased to have deduced something cleverly by himself. "The gold pillars must lead to the golden door. That's where the ring will be!" He didn't like the look of the stone door. A horde of mummies was probably waiting behind it. So, keen to crack on and get out of the Tomb of Doom, Mr Penguin leapt. He jumped before any of his friends could stop him and before Colin could say DON'T! WE NEED TO LOOK IN EDITH'S BOOK THIS COULD BE A TRICK.

Mr Penguin landed in a skiddy fashion on the first golden pillar then discovered it had, of course, been a trick.

CLUNK.

The pillar he was standing on jolted downwards, making Mr Penguin stumble about wildly with his flippers windmilling around his head. There was a fizz and a loud gushing noise from below. Mr Penguin looked down and yelped.

Underneath him, bubbling up at

speed, was a sea of red-hot lava.
"GREAT CRAB CAKES!"
he cried, jumping to the next
pillar. This one was gold too
and again it jolted
downwards, making
the lava rise more
quickly.

STOP JUMPING!
said Colin's pad.

Farooq quickly
found the translated
clues again in Edith's
notebook.

"ROOM TWO: ALL
THAT GLITTERS
ISN'T GOLD," he
read. "It's a trick.
We need to use the
stone pillars!"

Colin, Farooq

and Agent Eyeball then leapt nimbly on to the first stone pillar. They held their breaths, but thankfully nothing happened. Edith's notebook was right. They leapt like gazelles to the next one and the next.

Meanwhile, Mr Penguin was still gripping on to his golden pillar and beneath him the lava continued to rise, spitting and hissing with a ferocious heat. The pillar started to sway and, looking down, Mr Penguin realised that the gold was starting to melt!

From the stone pillar nearby his friends encouraged him to jump, but he couldn't. His legs had turned to jelly. But he knew if he stayed where he was he'd end up like a little penguin crouton in a bowl of boiling lava soup. The pillar swayed again and sank further into the boiling lava. Mr Penguin gritted his beak. He'd have to give it a go. He waddled

as fast as he could across the top of the
pillar. He squeezed his eyes shut. He
jumped.

He… smacked straight into the
wobbling stone pillar his friends were
balancing on. CLONK!

"Hold on, Mr Penguin!" cried
Farooq, and Mr Penguin did. He held
on as best as he could with his sweaty
flippers. Meanwhile, Colin leapt into
action. He clambered down to his friend
and tied a length of bum-web around his
belly… but instead
of leaping back up
to hurl his friend
to safety, he dived

into Mr Penguin's satchel and rummaged around.

"I don't think now is the time for a fish finger sandwich!" said Mr Penguin, although he would have dearly liked a nibble himself. Colin reappeared not with a sandwich, but with a date from the bottom of Mr Penguin's bag. Now, Colin leapt back up to the top of the wobbling pillar. He stuck the date to the floor and stood on top of it. The stickiness glued him to the spot and stopped him from sliding

about. He heaved and heaved. Farooq
and Agent Eyeball helped too – and
slowly (after he had been told to stop
being a plonker and let go of the pillar)
Mr Penguin was pulled to safety.

The Adventurers wasted no time,
leaping from one stone pillar to the next.
Mr Penguin wasn't the best jumper – he
sort of just splatted on to each stepping
stone – but it did the job.

The lava was very high now, and
several of the pillars had sunk into it.
They had one more leap to the door.
Suddenly there was a deafening crunch
and their pillar wobbled madly about.
It had split in half! Any moment now it
would tumble into the boiling bubbles
below.

Colin once again jumped into
action. He got Agent Eyeball to use her
to tail to fling him at the wall above the

stone door, which she did with great speed. Colin sailed through the air, holding the sticky date tightly with some of his leg-arms. SPLAT! The date stuck to the chamber wall and Colin stuck to it. Then he swirled a lasso of web around his head and hurled it so it caught Mr Penguin, Farooq and Agent Eyeball tight.

JUMP! said Colin's pad.

And they did, just as the pillar crumbled into the lava beneath them. They flew through the air straight towards the door.

"I HOPE IT ISN'T LOCKED!" cried Mr Penguin.

CHAPTER TWENTY-FOUR

YOUR TIME IS ALMOST UP

The door wasn't locked, thank goodness, and they sailed through with Colin following them. They rolled along the sandy floor and with a loud bang, the stone door slammed shut behind them. Lava gurgled around the doorframe, sealing it tightly closed. There was no way back.

Mr Penguin lay face down for a moment or two. His heart was thumping, his legs felt like they were made from mashed potato and he was feeling a bit sheepish. Once again he had tried to help, but it hadn't gone to plan and his friend had had to come to his rescue. His flipper sneaked into his bag and he gulped down the leftover fish finger sandwich, carpet fluff and all. MUCH BETTER. Then he rolled on to his back and opened his eyes.

"OH!" he gasped. He blinked a few times before believing where he was. He was inside an enormous pyramid. Slowly, the Adventurers realised that the rooms and tunnels they had been in so far must have been part of a huge underground network, which now opened up into one of the giant pyramids in the Valley of Peril. The four sides stretched up and joined at a point high above him.

Mr Penguin looked about. The entire room glittered and sparkled and gleamed with treasures. Huge golden statues of ancient gods and goddesses loomed above them, and piles of precious objects and jewels shone in the light of Farooq's torch. It was like being inside a beautiful treasure chest.

But Mr Penguin groaned.

Edith's notebook had said there were three tasks to complete and they had done two already: the sarcophagus room and the lava chamber. What awful thing faced them now? Would it be something from the book he and Colin had been reading – monsters and mummies? He shuddered, but heaved himself to his feet.

Farooq checked his pocket watch. Their time was almost up. They had five minutes to complete their task and rescue Edith and Gordon from being thrown into that pit.

The pyramid was so vast that the small halo of light made by Farooq's fading torch only lit up small circles of it at a time, which made looking for the Sun Stone ring incredibly tricky. There was so much stuff, and all of it shimmered and glistened.

The ticking clock, combined with his worries, had become too much for Mr Penguin.

"This is IMPOSSIBLE!" he said. "We'll never find it!"

Colin tapped his ankle, but Mr Penguin continued to gabble: "We won't, I know it!" He was really in a flap now.

Colin tapped him again.

"I mean," twittered Mr Penguin, "why couldn't this ring just be sitting on a nice table, all on its own, right next to me?"

At this Colin walloped Mr Penguin on the bottom with his notebook. Mr Penguin read Colin's pad.

IT IS it said.

Agent Eyeball pointed with her tail and Mr Penguin spun around.

And there it was, just as he'd said.

In the centre of the room was a small wooden table. Sitting on it was a little lead box. It was open and inside was the Sun Stone ring.

The Adventurers gathered around it. This was it? All the fuss and danger for this? Everything else in the room was sparkly, but the ring was just a dull metal band with what looked like a marble on top.

Farooq and Mr Penguin looked at it through their magnifying glasses. It looked like fire was burning inside the small jewel.

"Do we just take it?" whispered Mr Penguin.

Colin frowned.

I DON'T LIKE THIS said his pad.

Next page:

I DON'T LIKE THIS AT ALL.

"Neither do I," said Farooq, and Agent Eyeball mewed in agreement. "It's too easy! After the other tasks, why would this ring be on a table for us to find as easy as anything?"

Nobody could think why. There didn't seem to be any boobytraps, or spikes or lava. There weren't any hidden trapdoors, it seemed, and the idea of a monster or a mummy being in this glittering room seemed very silly indeed. Nevertheless, Farooq, Agent Eyeball and Colin paced around the table with the ring on it like sneaky panthers, their eyes darting about looking for hidden tricks and secret shenanigans. Mr Penguin just stood anxiously hopping from foot to foot.

A voice broke the silence. It was Cynthia again, her mean-sounding cackle echoing through the chamber. "TICK TOCK!" she hooted. "YOUR TIME IS ALMOST UP, MR PENGUIN!"

Mr Penguin gulped. The image of Edith and Gordon dangling over that awful pit filled his head. His friends

needed him. He'd made lots of silly
decisions in the tomb, but not saving them
wasn't going to be one of them.

"WE'VE FOUND IT!" shouted
Mr Penguin, then to his friends he said:
"Come on!"

He reached out and grabbed the
box, snapping it shut.

"BE CAREFUL!" cried Farooq and
Colin's pad said: GASP!

The Adventurers stood frozen to the
spot, waiting for whatever boobytrap would
be set off. They held their breaths.

But nothing happened. Nothing at all.

"Let's skedaddle!" whispered Farooq.

But where was the door? How would
they escape?

And it was then that there came a
sound from above them.

PING! FIZZ!

WATCH OUT! said Colin's pad.

Mr Penguin ducked as an arrow fired from a hidden crossbow flew through the air. It only just missed him, landing with a thud and a judder in to a large golden statue.

THERE'S A NOTE ON IT! said Colin's pad, and he held up a scroll of parchment.

They unrolled it and Farooq, using Edith's notebook, translated the hieroglyphics.

It said:

YOU HAVE BEEN WARNED.

And then a huge section of the wall in front of them slid open.

CHAPTER TWENTY-FIVE

YOU'VE GOT IT ALL WRONG

It was hard to tell who was more surprised to see each other – Mr Penguin and his pals or Cynthia and her crooks.

It turned out that the room full of gold and the Sun Stone ring was only separated from Edith, Gordon and the pit by the stone wall that had slid rather dramatically into the ground.

Edith's brothers Bernard and Jasper gasped when they saw the treasures piled high in the pyramid beyond. They tossed Edith and Gordon to the ground (thankfully not into the pit) and bounded in like lambs to investigate it all. They greedily filled their pockets with all the jewel-encrusted objects they could get their mitts on.

Cynthia, however, ignored the riches and ran over to Mr Penguin.

"GIVE IT TO ME," she said.

Beside her, Professor Umlaut squeaked, "Perhaps say please?" and Cynthia walloped him with her handbag.

Mr Penguin was handing the box over when Edith yelled: "Stop!" but her twin didn't listen. She reached out and plucked the ring from the box, holding it up to the light of Farooq's torch.

The Sun Stone seemed now to be

glowing. A red light flickered over
Cynthia's grinning face. The effect was,
Mr Penguin thought, terribly dramatic
but actually not very nice.

"The Sun Stone ring!" hissed
Cynthia in awe. "A gift from the Sun
God and now it's mine! ALL MINE!"
She cackled outrageously.

By now Edith, with Gordon on
her head, had run into the pyramid
room.

"No, Cynthia," she said, in a very
serious voice. "You've got it all wrong—"

But Cynthia wasn't listening. She
cried "ALL MINE!" again and thrust
it on to one of her fingers. She stood
admiring it from every angle.

Beside him, Mr Penguin heard
Edith muttering, "Oh dear! Oh dear!
Oh dear!"

Colin tapped him on the flipper

and held up his pad.

I'VE GOT A BAD FEELING ABOUT THIS it said, and Mr Penguin agreed.

Looking down he realised that his knees were knocking so badly it looked like he was doing a jig.

Cynthia ferreted around in her handbag, pulled out a small notebook and quickly thumbed through it. Then, reading from it, she uttered an ancient incantation.

"Uh oh…" muttered Edith, as the Sun Stone on Cynthia's finger began to glow fiercely.

Throwing the book back into her handbag, Cynthia, with wild, greedy eyes, reached out and touched the first thing she saw. It was the ornate wooden table the ring box had been sitting on.

Mr Penguin had to rub his eyes with his flippers to make sure what he was seeing was real. The moment Cynthia's hand touched its surface, rich, gleaming gold fanned out from her fingertips and ran like ink. Seconds later the whole table had been transformed into solid, shimmering gold.

Cynthia cackled gleefully and began touching anything she could see – Edith's notebook, her handbag, the briefcase Professor Umlaut had been lugging about with him. Instantly each object turned into a priceless treasure.

"Can't you see how excellent this is?" she cried. "And how rich I will be? Everything I own will be bright, brilliant gold! I'll have great vats of treasures! I'll be able to dive and swim through it all!"

Mr Penguin was going to say that he thought that sounded like a lot of hard work and as if it might hurt a bit, but he suddenly became aware that the floor beneath his feet was shaking. There was, from outside the pyramid, an incredible roll of thunder. The effect of both of these things was quite alarming.

He tapped Edith on the bumbag.

"Um, you know you said that Cynthia had got it all wrong?" he whispered, without taking his eyes from Cynthia who was skipping around the room, a trail of newly golden objects in her wake. "What did you mean by that?"

"She HAS got it all wrong," sighed Edith. "She didn't translate the story of the Sun Stone properly OR find the second half of the story! She always was slapdash with her homework."

Mr Penguin nodded. He was bubbling with worry. Thunder boomed again outside and the floor was still quaking.

Edith continued:

"The pharaoh wasn't given the Sun Stone ring from the Sun God. That's what Cynthia got wrong. Oh dear! Oh dear!"

There was an enormous clap of thunder and the entire room lit up as a bright white lightning bolt hit the tip of the pyramid, shattering the top stones and hurling them into the room. A chunk the size of a refrigerator landed right beside Mr Penguin – it would have flattened him entirely if Colin hadn't KAPOW-ed him out of the way.

Mr Penguin straightened his hat.

"What did happen?" he asked Edith.

"The pharaoh STOLE the ring and when the Sun God found out he was very, VERY angry! And now–" Another crackle of lightning shot like a javelin from the sky into the room.

"Now," she continued, "he wants REVENGE!"

CHAPTER TWENTY-SIX

THUNDER AND LIGHTNING

"Revenge?" cried Mr Penguin. "Yes!" yelled Edith over the noise of thunder and the trembling floor. "The Sun God found the greedy pharaoh and, well, look!" She pointed across the room.

Cynthia stopped twirling around the room turning things to gold and stood in the centre of the pyramid. Above her, the sky was visible through the hole in the roof. The sun blazed burning hot, yet the sky around it had turned a dark, dangerous-looking green.

Bernard and Jasper stopped filling their pockets with treasures and goggled. Professor Umlaut whimpered. Cynthia, it seemed, hadn't noticed. She was gazing at the ring on her finger and muttering, "I'll have a golden mansion, and a golden swimming pool and a library of golden books..."

Mr Penguin watched her and as another lightning bolt lit up the room, his eyes focused on a statue behind her. It was of a golden pharaoh, but instead of the rather stiff-looking statues elsewhere in the tomb, this one looked like the

sculptor had caught the king looking
horrified by something on his hand.
What it was, Mr Penguin couldn't think,
but then it all became awfully clear.

"Cynthia!" he cried. "Take that
ring off!"

Colin added THIS INSTANT!

But she didn't.

"No!" she shouted. "It's mine!"

"But it isn't!" said Farooq. "It
doesn't belong to you!"

Just then another bolt of lightning
crackled into the room and hit the Sun
Stone on Cynthia's finger. She stumbled
backwards a few steps but didn't seem
to be injured. The stone began to glow.
Yellow. Orange. Red. Then a bright,
brilliant, burning white.

"Ouch!" yelped Cynthia. "It's
actually gone very hot!"

Mr Penguin gulped. Getting very

hot wasn't the only thing it was doing. As he watched, he saw Cynthia's fingernail turn gold. Then the top of her finger. Then her entire finger.

"SHE'S TURNING INTO SOLID GOLD!" cried Mr Penguin, and it was true! Another finger on Cynthia's hand started to change too, and Mr Penguin realised that the statue of the pharaoh behind her wasn't a statue – it was the real pharaoh, magically transformed. That's what would happen to Cynthia.

She blinked, realising it too. It was as if she was waking up from a not-very-nice dream.

"HELP!" she cried. She started tugging at the ring, but Mr Penguin could see that she couldn't get it off.

"We must rescue her!" said Edith, determinedly.

As one, Edith and Gordon, Farooq, Colin, and Agent Eyeball ran over to Cynthia, with Mr Penguin waddling behind saying, "Oh my cod!" several times under his breath. The gold had covered three fingers now and Cynthia was starting to run about, doing a panicky dance not dissimilar to Mr Penguin's own.

"Stop panicking!" said Edith.

"We'll save you!" said Farooq.

But how would they get the ring off her hand?

WIGGLE IT! said Colin's pad and

Farooq grabbed hold of Cynthia's elbow and jiggled it like mad. At first nothing happened – the ring was stuck fast – but suddenly it flew through the air. It landed with a clink on the ground and great inky splodges of gold appeared wherever it rolled.

"Quick, Mr Penguin!" cried Edith. "Get it back in its box!"

Obediently, Mr Penguin hopped over and around the hissing golden puddles on the floor, but the ring was rolling all over the place. The entire tomb was trembling and shaking now.

The golden puddles spread across the flagstones and where they lapped up against the treasures and statues in the room, the objects began to sizzle and melt like wax.

Thunder boomed overhead and lightning flashed. Still Mr Penguin chased after the ring. Eventually it rolled into a dip in the ground. He went to grab it, but before he could, a paper aeroplane made from a sheet of paper from Colin's pad hit him on the beak.

He opened it.

DON'T TOUCH IT WITH YOUR FLIPPER (P.T.O.)

(Mr Penguin knew that meant Please Turn Over so he did)

YOU PLONKER!

Mr Penguin gasped. Colin was right. If he touched it he would turn to gold himself! How was he going to get the ring into the box? He quivered and tried to think. If only he was super clever like Edith or Farooq. He rummaged in his bag for anything that could help. His book? No. His lunchbox? No. His magnifying glass? No!

What about his umbrella?

Yes! That would work! He pierced the ring with the end of his brolly and carefully manoeuvred it into the metal box. The tip of umbrella started to turn a bit gold, but as soon as the ring was in the box Mr Penguin slammed the lid shut.

But their troubles weren't over.

CHAPTER TWENTY-SEVEN

ABSOLUTE CALAMITY

Mr Penguin turned around, holding the ring box triumphantly above his head. He'd done it! He'd saved the day! But instead of being greeted by cheering from his friends, he found a scene of absolute calamity.

The gold had turned from puddles to great lakes and was now rapidly becoming a sea. The pit where Edith and Gordon had been dangled was now overflowing with hot, gloopy molten gold.

The islands made from the fallen stone slabs were few and far between and Mr Penguin was alone, with his friends and the crooks all madly climbing on to another bigger slab nearby. He tucked the metal ring box into his bag for safety.

I THINK WE NEED TO LEAVE NOW said Colin's pad. HEAD TO THE DOOR.

And he helpfully drew an arrow pointing to the entrance chamber… just as a large stone slid from the ceiling and sealed it up.

Mr Penguin gasped, nearly falling from his slab. It was hard to stay upright on it as it was bobbling about on the sizzling golden sea that was rising higher and higher.

Mr Penguin looked around. How WERE they going to leave? The stairs were sealed and the door the Adventurers had stumbled through earlier was glued up with a great bubbling vat of lava. They were trapped!

"This is the third task!" said Farooq. He turned to Edith. Her notebook had been turned to solid gold by her sister, but she must know how they could escape? But she shook her head.

It was, of all people, Gordon who came up with the solution. He had been sleeping peacefully through everything on top of Edith's head, but now he woke up, looked around and, with one of his foghorn-like honks, fluttered up to the open tip of the pyramid.

Of course! If they couldn't leave by

any of the doors, they would have to leave
from the roof!

"Quickly!" cried Edith.

"I think this place is going to
explode like a volcano!" cried Farooq,
and he wasn't wrong. The gold was
bubbling all around and rising higher
and higher and HIGHER. Beneath, in
the depths of the tomb, there were deep
angry grumbling noises that Mr Penguin

wasn't at all thrilled to hear.

By wobbling carefully and with
determination, they managed to rock
the two stone rafts to the outer edges of
the room. Here some of the enormous
golden statues were still just about
standing, although sizzles and hisses said
that they too were beginning to melt.

Agent Eyeball nimbly jumped
up on to the gigantic gleaming statue
of a god with the head of an alligator.
She was followed by Farooq, Colin and
Edith, who helped Bernard, Jasper and
Professor Umlaut scramble up too.
The two brothers and the professor
were all looking distinctly peaky. Their
earlier bluster had vanished and they
were absolutely terrified. Mr Penguin
understood how they felt. His legs felt
like cooked spaghetti and his stomach
rumbled with nervous hunger.

He and Cynthia were the last to clamber up on to the statue. Carefully the group climbed up to the ornate headdress and then Colin threw out a lasso of bum-web, hooking it on to the lip of the broken tip of the pyramid. He scuttled up it and helped heave the group to safety: first the Adventurers and then the crooks. Mr Penguin heard their footsteps slipping and sliding on the outside of the pyramid.

Finally, the only ones left were Mr Penguin and Cynthia. Mr Penguin was a polite penguin and insisted, despite his nerves, that Cynthia go first. He helped her up, all the time keeping one wild eye on the bubbling golden lava beneath him which was hissing and rising at an alarming rate. Eventually, Cynthia heaved herself out of the pyramid (not easy with one golden hand) and Mr Penguin reached up for the length of web.

"In a moment I will be safe," muttered Mr Penguin. "Safe and on my way to get a little nibble to eat!" He grinned, and Colin grinned back encouragingly. Above him, the clouds swirled in the eerie, dark green sky.

Then there was confusion: the sound of footsteps running UP the outside of the pyramid. The building groaned and rocked. Lightning flashed. Colin suddenly disappeared and so did his web rope.

Cynthia's face appeared above Mr Penguin.

"Oh thank goodness!' cried Mr Penguin. "I thought I was going to be trapped in here!"

He reached up for Cynthia's hand. She stretched out. And then the unbelievable happened.

Instead of grasping his flipper, she

slapped it out of the way. She grabbed hold of his satchel instead and rifled through it. Then she pulled out the ring box and held it triumphantly above her head.

"I TOLD YOU THE SUN STONE WOULD BE MINE!" she hissed.

CHAPTER TWENTY-EIGHT

THE END OF
MR PENGUIN?

"BYE BYE, MR PENGUIN!"
cried Cynthia.

Mr Penguin couldn't believe it.
After everything, Cynthia still wanted
the ring! And now here he was on a
rapidly disappearing safe spot in a
pyramid that was about to explode.

It felt as if the entire tomb had come to life and was doing everything it could to keep him trapped inside. The place trembled powerfully, making the giant alligator's head shudder and shake.

Above him, Cynthia laughed a not-very-nice laugh and turned on her heel, but lightning flashed again and the building shook more violently than ever.

"Cynthia!" shouted Mr Penguin. "Um, please can you help me?"

Cynthia turned back to say something, and that was her mistake. The pyramid quivered under her feet and with a gasp, she fell back into the pyramid!

She landed heavily next to Mr Penguin on the alligator's head. Mr Penguin wasn't sure what to say so he just said, "Hello!"

Then the panic struck him. Here he was in his worst nightmare. He was trapped in a pyramid, not with a mummy but with a terrible villain, and he had no way out. The rope was gone, none of his friends were there to help him and he felt utterly useless. No clever Edith, no weird but brilliantly useful Gordon, no detective Farooq and no super-brave Colin. If his gang had been with him, they'd have had an idea put together in seconds.

Think, Mr Penguin! Think! he told himself. There must be a way out of here. The alternative was – well, it didn't bear thinking about really.

"DO SOMETHING, YOU IDIOT!" commanded Cynthia, and to his surprise Mr Penguin said, "Pipe down, I'm thinking!" which felt like a very brave thing to do.

Brave like Colin.

Spurred on by this thought he decided to try to be clever like Edith and

Farooq. It was difficult to do with golden lava lapping at his toes and the statue under his feet melting and shuddering dangerously.

But think he did, and he realised that actually he hadn't been entirely useless. Yes, he'd caused some hairy moments in the tomb, but he had cleverly used his umbrella to hook the ring up and shut it up tight in its box.

Hang on! Could his umbrella help again?

He looked up and realised that yes it could! The boiling hot, churning lake of liquid gold was rising, so the hole at the top of the pyramid was now only JUST out of reach.

He hoiked the brolly out of his bag and, by jumping as high as he could, he managed to hook the handle over the edge of the hole above him. He heaved himself up and out, feeling cool air on his handsome hat.

"HEY! WADDABOUT ME?" shouted Cynthia from inside the pyramid-volcano.

Now, if Mr Penguin had been a different sort of penguin, he might have left the dangerous and sly villain there, but he didn't. Mr Penguin was a Jolly Nice Sort so, turning the umbrella round, he stretched the handle out to help Cynthia.

"GRAB IT!" he cried.

Cynthia tried, but her palms were too sweaty.

Mr Penguin rummaged around in his bag again and found the last sticky date. He stuck it to the handle before offering it to Cynthia again.

She grabbed it with her half golden hand – in the other she was gripping like

a vice on to the ring box
with the Sun Stone inside.

The golden alligator
statue swayed as it began to
dissolve into the molten
metal surrounding it.
Cynthia had a devil of
a job to stop herself
falling.

"LEAVE THE RING!" said Mr
Penguin, but Cynthia shouted, "NO!
NEVER! My riches! My golden mansion!"

Mr Penguin couldn't believe it.
Surely none of those things mattered? But
they did to Cynthia. Her eyes were wild
again, wild and flashing with greed. She
simply wouldn't let go. What could he do?

Then suddenly – an idea! As quick
as a flash, he tugged his umbrella and
walloped the ring box out of her hand.

It flew through the air, landed with

a heavy SPLOSH on to the bubbling gold liquid and vanished into it with a hiss.

Cynthia cried, "NOOOOOOOOO!" and went to jump in after it, but Mr Penguin hooked the handle of his brolly into the neck of her blouse and heaved with all his might, pulling her to safety. With an ear-splitting hiss, the alligator statue melted into the seething lake of gold lava.

Together, Mr Penguin and Cynthia tumbled down the side of the pyramid and bounced across the sand.

And they were just in time.

The pyramid erupted like a volcano.

CHAPTER TWENTY-NINE

A LAST BIT OF
KNEE KNOCKING

The explosion lasted for several long minutes. Droplets of gold rained down on the Valley of Peril and Mr Penguin was, not for the first time, very pleased that he had his umbrella with him to protect himself from the storm.

And then it was over.

From their hiding place behind a ruined temple, everyone watched as the dark green sky cleared and the pyramid they had just escaped from vanished into the sand. Soon there was nothing left apart from a mess of scattered golden flakes and the crumbled remains of old stone.

For a minute nobody said or did anything, then they came to their senses. The crooks tried to scarper, but Colin was ready for them. In an instant he had bound them up tightly with an extra-strong strand of his bum-web. He collared Professor Umlaut, who had been dithering about whether to run or not.

"I didn't want to be a part of this!" Umlaut wailed. "SHE MADE ME!"

Farooq and Edith went through the crooks' pockets and a large number of treasures were soon piled up in the cool shadowy nook they had found to shelter in.

Edith tutted at the heap and her siblings scowled.

Mr Penguin didn't help with any of

this. He was too busy lying face down on the floor, exhausted.

Edith and the rest of the gang plumped themselves down beside him and eventually coaxed him upright with a cookie Edith found in her bumbag. It wasn't a fish finger sandwich, but it would do.

"What a morning!" sighed Farooq as Agent Eyeball curled up on his lap. "What a few days, actually!"

A lot certainly had happened. Now, in the calmness away from the Tomb of Doom, Edith slowly told them again how she had been on the case. How she had read in Cynthia's new book about the Sun Stone ring, but, by doing her own studies, realised that Cynthia hadn't got it quite right and was missing quite an important part of the story.

"The pharaoh who stole the ring used

its power for evil – he lived in a golden palace whilst all the people in his kingdom suffered dreadfully. When his crimes were discovered, the Sun God punished him terribly. I found out that this place," she pointed to where the pyramid had stood, "would be chockful of boobytraps. The ancient people who built it wanted to ensure that nobody would ever find the ring again."

AND IT WAS SEEING DR FOSSIL'S MUSEUM IN THE NEWSPAPER THAT MADE YOU SUSPICIOUS? said Colin's pad, and Edith nodded.

"Yes," she said gravely. "I'd hoped when my brothers both changed their surnames from Hedge that they had put all their naughtiness behind them – that they'd become new, better people. I tried to keep an eye on them from afar, but it

wasn't always easy – particularly with
Jasper. When I saw Bernard's name
in the newspaper I was immediately
interested. He didn't let it be known that
his amulet had been stolen, but I got
right into investigating that, and I started
to connect the dots."

Farooq said that two things
were still puzzling him. "What I don't
understand is how you knew that your
amulets were the key to open the
tomb?" he said. "And you said that you
scampered out here on your own mission
– what was that?"

Edith grinned her cheeky grin, but
before she could answer, Mr Penguin
gulped down the last of his cookie, and
sighed happily. "I'm just glad that all this
is over and we
didn't have to deal
with any monsters or

cursed mumm—"

He broke off with a gasp, one of his flippers outstretched and quivering.

Although the sun was shining, the strange chill wind still blew through the Valley of Peril. It made the sand fly up in billowing clouds. The feathers on Mr Penguin's neck stood up on end.

His friends turned to look.

A shadow had been thrown on to a nearby wall. Something was moving slowly towards them.

Soon the sound of shuffling footsteps was heard and a low, worried moaning.

"MUMMY!" cried Mr Penguin. "AN ANCIENT MUMMY IS COMING TO GET US!"

Then Edith said, "That's not an ancient mummy, Mr Penguin..." as whatever it was came staggering out of the shadows and into the light.

CHAPTER THIRTY

THE MUMMY
RETURNS

"What?" said Mr Penguin.

"I said, 'It's not AN ancient mummy, Mr Penguin'," said Edith. "It's MY ancient mummy!"

But before she could explain, Mr Penguin fainted.

He came to a few minutes later and found himself looking not into the eyes of a bandaged, mummified face, but the smile of a very, very elderly woman. A woman who looked remarkably like Edith.

"He'll be OK," said the woman. "Dr Dorothea Ermentrude Hedge!" she continued, shaking his flipper very firmly indeed. "Sorry if I startled you," she said heartily. "Shuffling about like that and moaning. I'd got some sand in my eye – and really, slippers aren't the best things to be hoofing about the desert in, but my goodness they are comfortable!" She wiggled her feet to show a pair of very fluffy slippers.

"I don't understand," said Mr Penguin. "This is your mum?"

He looked at Edith. Edith was rather

old, so goodness knows how old her
mum must be!

"Oh yes!" said Edith cheerfully.
"Dear old Mother. She's 105 years old
and still being an archaeologist."

"Of course," said Dr Hedge. "You
have to keep busy!"

Quickly, Edith filled her in on
everything that had happened.

"Mother is the one who realised
that the amulets might be the key to
the tomb," continued Edith. "She's
always been sure that they were more
important than she first thought. She'd
located the tomb, too, and that's why I
was hurrying here. I was coming to warn
her that we had been right – Cynthia
WAS behind it all."

"I'm just sorry I'm so late," said
Dr Hedge. "I had trouble with my
camels." She pointed to the top of a

nearby sand dune where a number of camels were resting grumpily.

Dr Hedge turned to the crooks, tied up and still sulking.

"Well, well, well..." she said. "All of you up to your old tricks again!"

"And Edith, little goody two shoes again!" said Cynthia.

"Edith is NOT a goody two shoes!" said Dr Hedge firmly. "I'll NEVER forget the time she bit off the bottom of an ice-cream cone and gave it to me as a joke. That chocolate sauce made SUCH a mess of my skirt!"

Mr Penguin, Farooq and Colin tittered at the thought of Edith doing such a thing.

"What Edith is, is kind. Something all the rest of you need to try being!" continued Dr Hedge. "Honestly – stealing! Opening lost tombs! I'm very disappointed in your behaviour, especially you Cynthia. And you, Umlaut, you knew it was wrong but you didn't try to stop it."

Professor Umlaut flushed pink.

"Now, I don't want any more chitter-chatter from you!" said Dr Hedge. "You know exactly what I'm going to say, don't you?"

The crooks looked sheepish.

"PARDON?" said Dr Hedge.

"If you make a mess you must clean it up!" mumbled the crooks.

Colin released them and let them start on the task of clearing up the site where the ancient tomb used to be.

Mr Penguin stood next to Dr Hedge and watched them closely.

"Cynthia was always so clever," sighed Dr Hedge. "Just like Edith, but she could never quite help being influenced by her brothers. Together they would all make such a good team, but they can't resist trouble. Well, hopefully this time they'll have learned their lesson. I'm going to keep them here with me where I can keep a close eye on them!"

She looked down at Mr Penguin.

"I'm glad Edith has jolly nice friends like you and Colin and Gordon," she said. "Now you ARE a good team."

Mr Penguin wasn't sure. He explained how he always felt a bit useless compared to his pals.

Dr Hedge laughed. "Nonsense!" she said. "You are every bit as clever and brave and useful as your chums. Look at how you saved the day all by yourself! And you got rid of that awful Sun Stone ring forever!"

"Only because I was thinking what my friends would do in that situation," said Mr Penguin.

"But that's what friends do – they help each other out. You even helped Cynthia when all she'd been was VERY badly behaved indeed. AND when you were feeling frightened in the tomb you never gave up, because you wanted to save Edith and Gordon. So really, Mr Penguin, you are clever and brave and useful AND kind."

Mr Penguin felt a lot better for hearing that and puffed his chest out with pride.

Just then Farooq ambled over.

"It's halfway through the day, Mr Penguin," he said. "If we want to get back to Laghaz before nightfall, we'll have to go now."

There was a great amount of fussing about as everyone gathered themselves. Colin helped Mr Penguin check he had all his things in his bag –

his magnifying glass, his gold-tipped brolly, his lunchbox and the library book. Edith hugged her mum goodbye and Gordon tried to eat a mouthful of sand. Before they left Dr Hedge rummaged around in her handbag, found a piece of paper and scribbled something on it, then pinned it to Farooq's tunic with his other badges.

It said:

Excellent Codebreaker and Detective.

"You were immensely brave and clever," she said. "And if you ever want to do some detecting of very old things, I'd love to have you on one of my archaeology teams!"

Farooq beamed and Agent Eyeball purred proudly. Then they were ready to go.

"Wait a moment!" said Mr Penguin, perplexed. "How are we going to get back to Laghaz?"

He spotted the pile of treasure.

"Oh!" he exclaimed. "Maybe we could use a bit of this to pay for a taxi to take us back?"

"A taxi? In the middle of the desert?" laughed Farooq.

Mr Penguin frowned. How else would they get back to the city? Then he realised and groaned.

"CAMELS?" he said.

"Camels!" said Farooq, giggling.

And so the Adventurers set off and, without any dates to stick his bum to the animal, Mr Penguin spent the entire journey trying his best to cling on to the wildly galloping beast.

He just hoped that when he got back to his hotel there was an enormous fish finger sandwich waiting for him.

In the Valley of Peril, deep inside a tomb, in an ancient sarcophagus, a beady eye opened and peeked through a crack in the bandages.

They had been resting there for thousands of years but today they had heard a lot of noise nearby that had woken them up.

The mummy sighed.

Should I get up and do some haunting? they thought to themselves.

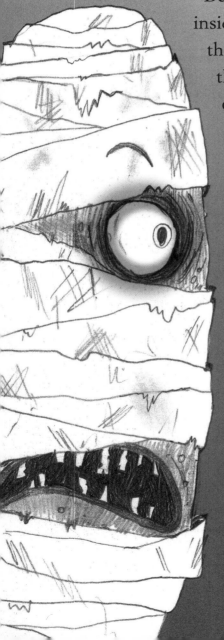

No.

Better to stay safely here inside this pyramid, they thought. You never know – there might be penguins outside…

And there is nothing more alarming than an unexpected penguin.

Laghaz Gazette

LOCAL BOY HAILED A HERO!

Boy, 10, Teams Up with World-Famous Detective to Trace Missing Woman

A local boy is being hailed a hero after he and his cat teamed up with a world-famous detective duo to solve the case of missing ancient scroll translator and pigeon enthusiast, Edith Hedge.

Farooq, 10, and his cat Iris, aka "Agent Eyeball", got in touch with Adventurer and Penguin Mr Penguin and his sidekick, Colin, when they realised that they might have some clues regarding the vanishing of Mr Penguin's friend Edith Hedge.

Over fish-finger sandwiches in a top Laghaz hotel, Farooq told the *Laghaz Gazette* how he and Agent Eyeball tracked Mr Penguin and Colin down, helped put the clues together and, after a short trek through the desert, found Edith Hedge and reunited her with her friends.

"I have been in training as a detective for months," said Farooq, tucking into his fifth sandwich, "and it was very exciting to be able to get stuck in on my very first case."

Agent Eyeball miaowed in agreement before licking tartare sauce off her whiskers.

But what happened to Edith Hedge? Where DID she go? The answer, it seems, is simple.

"It was a case of misunderstanding," explained Edith Hedge, adjusting her bumbag. "I went to visit my mother, who is a famous archaeologist, but unfortunately my note explaining this was eaten by my pet pigeon, Gordon, so Mr Penguin and Colin didn't know what had happened. It was very nice of them to come and find me though."

"Yes," said Mr Penguin, "and I tell you what – absolutely nothing scary or weird happened in the desert at all!" He then laughed nervously for five minutes.

WEIRD WEATHER IN DESERT REMAINS UNEXPLAINED

A strange and sudden storm over the desert still has experts baffled today as they search for ideas as to what caused the commotion.

Great green storm clouds were reported yesterday along with a frenzied bout of lightning and thunder culminating in a sudden explosion.

What caused it all is still very much a mystery.

BRIGHT FUTURE AHEAD FOR FAROOQ

It seems there is a bright future ahead for local heroes Farooq and Agent Eyeball, with not one but TWO jobs offered to them just today.

Farooq's older brother, a detective in the Laghaz police force, has offered his brother a job as a Junior Detective In Training after being impressed by his sibling's bravery and clue-solving skills.

Farooq and Agent Eyeball will be taking up the position after the school holidays, during which they will be working on Farooq's second job offer – Archaeologist's Assistant, under the leadership of Edith Hedge's mother, Dr Hedge.

THANK YOU TO:
DETECTIVE/PENGUIN
RACHEL WADE,
EDITOR-IN-CHIEF
AND
DETECTIVE/PENGUIN
ALISON STILL,
DESIGNER
PAR EXCELLENCE

SPECIAL THANKS TO:
DETECTIVE/PENGUIN AMINA YOUSSEF FOR HER EXCELLENT AND WONDERFUL ADVICE ON ALL THINGS EGYPTIAN.

Detectives/Penguins Tamlyn Francis, Caroline Thomson and Alison Eldred, Super Agents

DETECTIVE/PENGUIN REBECCA LOGAN AND DETECTIVE/PENGUIN EMILY FINN FOR THEIR EXPERT PR AND MARKETING SKILLS.